Mary Brewster's Love Life

Matriarch of the *Mayflower*

By Kathryn Brewster Haueisen

MARY BREWSTER'S
LOVE LIFE
Matriarch of the Mayflower

KATHRYN BREWSTER HAUEISEN

Kathryn Brewster Haueisen

Mary Brewster's
Love Life / Matriarch of the *Mayflower*
Copyright © 2023
by Kathryn Brewster Haueisen

Ordering Information:
Special discounts available for **book clubs, corporations, associations**.
For details, contact the publisher at director@vanvelzerpress.com.

The characters and events in this book are a fictional account of actual historical events and people. The author does not claim them to be historically accurate.

Paperback ISBN: 978-1-954253-30-8
Hardback ISBN: 978-1-954253-31-5
eBook ISBN: 978-1-954253-32-2
Library of Congress Control Number Available from Publisher

Printed in the United States of America
FSC-certified paper when possible

Van Velzer Press
Brandon, Vermont 05733
(802) 247-6797

VanVelzerPress.com

To the people that have encouraged me
through the
numerous transitions of my life.

Dear Reader,

I trust that since you have chosen to add this book to your To Be Read list, you may be an enthusiast of all things related to the remarkable story of the Pilgrims who settled in the Cape Cod area in 1620. Today there are millions who claim kinship to one or more of the passengers on the *Mayflower*. I claim ancestry to Elder William and Mary Brewster. Until I started doing research about her more famous husband, I knew virtually nothing about her.

Whenever anyone in the family spoke of our connection to the Brewster family, it was always about Elder Brewster. Mary was merely a necessary part of the connection from William through the generations to my generation and beyond. As I got to know her better, I became rather fond of Mary. What a life she lived! There is still much we don't know, and perhaps never will. Thus, I have written a fictional biography based on extensive research and much traveling to the places mentioned. We know where and when she went to these areas; they are recorded by history. We also know who she went with, and what happened along the path from Scrooby (England) to Amsterdam to Leyden, and finally to Cape Cod. Today the lovely city in The Netherlands is spelled Leiden. When Mary lived there is was spelled Leyden.

We know how many children she had and approximately when they were born. We have good guesses about when she was married and when each of her children married. Other details are ambiguous and subject to debate. Proven facts remain elusive. So, please, don't use this book for your genealogy research!

I've provided resources for that at the end.

Rather, think about all she sacrificed, all she endured, all her internal and external struggles as a wife and especially as a loving mother. Connect that with your ancestors, what their lives were like during this time in history. Imagine yourself walking in their steps. If you're married, would you truly follow your husband anywhere? *Anywhere on earth?* If you're a mother, can you fathom the pain of deciding to leave three of your five children behind, on the other side of an ocean?

With no phones!

All the diary entries and most of the conversations are fictional, however, many are based on documents that survived through the centuries. We don't know if Mary knew how to read and write. A few women in her era did; most did not. Her correspondence with others is fictional. For the sake of easier reading for you, dear reader, I've told her story in modern English with a smattering of the old style for flavor, though this is not how she would have spoken and written. Some of the dates are my best estimates about an event. I have been faithful to all the facts I could find, yet some contradict one another, depending on whose research I used.

This is not a history book; rather it is a glimpse into the heart, mind and soul of a woman who faithfully provided decades of strength and encouragement to a man who was a legend in his day and beyond. It is a story of one woman whose capacity to love and nurture expanded far beyond her own children.

This is the story of a woman who knew how to give unconditional love.

Welcome to the love life of Matriarch Mary Brewster. I proudly claim her as my ancestor.

Kathryn Brewster Haueisen

May 1, 1627

My name is Fear Allerton. Elder William and Mary Brewster are my parents. In the years since 1623 when I joined them here at Plimoth Plantation, until I married Isaac Allerton last year, I lived with them in their cottage. Mother told me many stories about her life and let me know that she kept a diary of her adventures. She didn't think anyone beyond myself, my sister Patience, and our brothers (Jonathan, Love and Wrestling) would be interested in her life.

She was wrong about that, so I have set forth to tell you her story, in her own words, as she told the remarkable events of her life to me in the years we lived together. I will also be adding parts of her diary in exactly her own words. I trust you may find her life as inspiring as I have. Some say she was brave. Others thought her foolish to sail away leaving us behind. As her daughter, I say she did what was expected of any respectable, proper Christian woman. She remained loyal to my father, even when that caused her pain as deep as the sea that separated us for years.

She did have choices. Other wives from our Leyden fellowship did not sail with their husbands. Other mothers didn't subject their young children to the dangers of the deep waters. Mother chose to follow our father wherever he felt guided by the Holy Ghost to go. When Mother died a few weeks ago she was the oldest woman here. In the end, I believe she simply wore out. Her life was a remarkable journey.

Here, in her own words, is her story . . .

Chapter 1

August 1, 1619

I love my husband, truly I do. I always have and I will until I breathe no more. But when the magistrates came last month to confiscate his things and arrest him, I was terrified. If they caught him, they may have hanged him. My hand still quivers recalling the details of the day. Now I am left alone to manage it all. If he were here I would . . . well, I do not know what I would do. It would not be pleasant. This is too much. How does he expect me to manage the mess left behind while he hides who knows where?! Thank the good Lord for the Robinsons. I truly do not know how I should cope without them.

~ ~ ~

I felt faint with fear when the magistrates came looking for William. I gripped the back of a chair to keep from falling to the ground. The room swayed around me. Their voices sounded far away as they shouted angry questions about where William was and what he was doing. After they left, and I had a moment to think about what just happened, I was furious at William for putting us in such a predicament. If the Dutch magistrates found him and returned him to England, I was certain they would execute him, leaving me a widow to raise five children, plus his cousin's orphaned children who lived with us then. That day brought a bitter stew of trouble into our home. Prior to that, our lives had for the most part been tranquil with just that one hurried move . . .

~ ~ ~

We went into exile to the Lowlands in 1608 with around a hundred others from our non-conformist Separatists fellowship around Scrooby, England. At first we didn't call ourselves Separatists as others did; but in time, we claimed that name for ourselves as well. We saw no hope for the Established Church of England and believed complete separation from it was necessary to be faithful to our Lord as we understand his claim on our lives. Other thought they could remain within the Established Church and purify it from within. They came to be known as Puritans.

At first, we went to Amsterdam because we knew hundreds of other English Separatists had settled there. Soon troubles there made us wonder if it might not have been better to take our chances in England. For a year William and Pastors Robinson and Clyfton tried to calm down the troubled waters among the factions. They made little progress. William told glorious stories about his earlier years in Leyden with Sir William Davison. In the short time William worked for Sir Davison, he often accompanied him on trips to the Lowlands when Sir Davison was Queen Elizabeth's ambassador. They especially enjoyed their time in Leyden, so that was chosen as our next home. We relocated to Leyden in 1609. Pastor Clyfton stayed in Amsterdam, hoping to help those arguing with one another to achieve peace.

Kathryn Brewster Haueisen

Pastor John Robinson became our pastor and the community appointed William our Elder, along with Samuel Fuller as a Deacon. Our family fared better than many due to a large extent because William had prior experience in Leyden. He remembered some of the Dutch tongue and soon found employment at the university teaching international students English.

I spent my days trying to learn the Dutch language, their customs and caring for Jonathan, Patience and Fear. I was already forty when we arrived in Leyden, yet the Lord blessed with me with another child. It pains me yet, all these years later, to think of that poor babe. He never took in a single breath.

I was still grieving for that babe when William announced we would be adding two orphan cousins of his to our home. William received word that a cousin's children in England were orphans. That's how Ann and Robert Pecke came to live with us.

"We cannot leave them helpless when we have been so abundantly blessed," he insisted when he learned of their plight. He sent the money to pay for their travel without consulting me.

Why would he? As the husband of our family, he made the decisions. Still, since the early days of our marriage, I was accustomed to him soliciting my thinking about a matter. So, I was angry at the way this came about. On this subject he made haste to settle the financial details for the Pecke orphans to come to our home in Leyden. *His place to decide. Mine place to adjust.*

Our home was full, but then the Lord gave me two more sons, Love in 1611 and Wrestling in 1614. Those days were challenging, but no more so than back in England. At least here we had less chance of being arrested for the way we worshiped.

By then Jonathan had moved into his own apartment. Along with Ann and Robert Pecke and my two little sons, I also had my daughters at home. I never lacked for something to do. We also had Buddy, a dog that followed the children home one day. They were so good about not complaining about our full house that I had not the heart to tell them no when they begged to keep Buddy. "As long as you understand that Buddy sleeps outside. I don't need to worry about tripping over a dog."

They promised.

I had to admit, Buddy actually made my load a little lighter. He was a medium black and white spaniel who would play fetch with them all day. He followed the children everywhere and kept them well entertained, freeing up my time.

~ ~ ~

Our home in Leyden was on an alley, which bore the unfortunate name of Stink Alley—*Stinksteeg* in Dutch. Is that not a fine kettle of fish for a name of street!? The alley earned its distasteful name because that is where people put their garbage, and it did stink nearly all the time. One door of our home opened onto Koorsteeg, which means Choir Alley in English and *Vicus Chorali* in Latin. Our home was a few paces away from Pieterskirk, a grand cathedral with a choir, so I suppose that is why Choir Alley was named as it was.

Our situation began to shift some time in 1617 when Thomas Brewer helped William set up a publishing business with help from Pastor Robinson and Edward Winslow, a young fellow originally from London. William decided to name his publishing business Choir Alley Press. Some days they worked up in our attic room from early morning until late in the evening. I rarely ventured into the room, except occasionally to take them a bit of refreshment. Every horizontal surface was piled high with books and loose papers. How they could work in such a mess amazed me; somehow, they managed. At first William and the others published English translations of books written by other theologians around Europe. Throughout 1618 they published many volumes, most of them of little interest to anyone beyond their circle of church leaders. However, they also thought it imperative to reprint several volumes against the Established Church of England. While I

Kathryn Brewster Haueisen

fully supported their objections to the excesses of the church, I would have preferred that William and his colleagues kept such opinions to themselves. He must have known I would disapprove.

I had little knowledge of what transpired right above my head in my own home.

William did speak vaguely about one volume he seemed particularly excited to print. It was a volume written by the Scottish Reverend David Calderwood, who was adamant in his protests against King James. William admitted to me one night over dinner that King James was furious with the things Reverend Calderwood wrote, but that didn't stop my William from printing copies. I think it excited William to participate in objecting to King James and his church in this way. I would often hear him say something like, "He thinks the church is his! I cannot believe his arrogance. He is worse than the Pope that he rails against."

In April 1619 they released a controversial book about a Perth Assembly and smuggled copies into England. At the time, I knew nothing of this. Apparently, I had already said too much, so William deemed it best to withhold details about what they did in the garret. I had plenty of worries of my own keeping our family fed and clothed. It was rare to have only our own family expecting a meal. William extended invitations to join us to many university students and church members who frequently dropped by.

That volume about the Perth Assembly proved too much for King James. He eventually figured out who was behind the dastardly diatribes and demanded the Dutch authorities confiscate all Choir Alley Press work. Official decrees further demanded the Dutch authorities send William back to England to face the consequences of defying King James. That is why the magistrates came to our home. That day ended my days of contentment. Some dates become permanently affixed in our memories: July 17, 1619 was such a day.

Chapter 2

July 17, 1619

This morning is a gorgeous day, one that makes me grateful to be alive. I think I shall take the children with me to market. They can help carry the lighter baskets and we can stop along the canal to feed the fish. They always love tossing breadcrumbs into the canal and watching the fish jump to get them.

It was a fresh day, the kind where I kept a shawl close at hand but took it off frequently. I was slowly making my way home from market with the younger children. Patience and Fear were at the house. Jonathan was at work. William was teaching at the university. I learned much later that some of his university friends heard rumors the magistrates sought to arrest him and warned him in time for him to get away.

It was one of the first cool days of summer and we were savoring the brisk air coming at us from the ocean, only a few kilometers away. We were in no hurry to return home. Shopping with four children slowed my progress; yet it also helped since all four were of sufficient age to carry a small basket. That enabled me to purchase enough to skip the next market day and save all of us precious time. The children were especially helpful that day, so we stopped along the canal. I rested on a bench and let them toss crumbs into the canal to watch the fish scramble to the surface after them. The sky was the color of robins' eggs and filled with brilliant fluffy clouds. When the children exhausted their supply of bread, they joined me. I told them I thought I saw a dog chasing a cat in the clouds.

Love pointed up. "I see a cow grazing."

"Mama, look, see, a horse and rider," said Wrestling.

Ann Pecke shook her little head so hard her blond hair flew in every direction. "There is a tiger! There. See?" How on earth the child knew what a tiger looked like mystified me. Perhaps she saw one in a book.

"Bloody fool," accused her brother Robert. "I see a dog chasing a cat too." It was like him to solicit special favor from me by supporting me.

Those few moments were the last peaceful ones I would know for many months. How quickly life turned from tranquil to tumultuous. I tucked away the memory of those precious few moments in a secret box within my heart. I pulled the memory out now and then when life threatened to overcome me, as it did often after that day. That memory gave me a bit of tranquility in the midst of troubles and sorrow. Pulling out sweet memories on sour days was a little game I played in my mind.

Robert and Love saw them first.

"Look!"

I followed their pointing fingers to see two men dressed in the official uniforms of the city knocking furiously on our door. Before I could reach the house, I saw the door open. As I approached, I collected all our baskets and sent the children down the alley, around the cathedral, to the Robinson home. "Tell Mrs. Robinson I shall come for you once I learn what these men want of us. Go straight there. Stay there until I come for you or I send Patience or Fear to fetch you. Go now."

Kathryn Brewster Haueisen

I waited until I was certain they were doing as directed. Then I hurried to see what was going on. Patience peered around the open door. I heard one of the men demanding of her, "Where is your father? Your mother?"

I said a quick prayer that I might keep my wits about me and called out to the men. "I am Mrs. Brewster. I've just returned from the shops." I reached around the fellows to hand the biggest basket to Patience. Then I walked ahead of the men into the house and turned to face them using the other baskets as a makeshift barrier. Fear cowered by the fireplace. Patience backed up to make room for me between her and the intruders.

"Fear, please go look after the children. I sent them to call on the Robinsons. Mrs. Robinson will welcome your assistance. Stay there until I come for you." Fear cautiously approached the door. The men stood aside to let her pass. When she was out in the street, she quickly disappeared down the alley.

The men turned to me, one of them waving a paper in my face. "We have orders with us to fetch Mr. Brewster. Hate to disrupt you, Mrs. Brewster, but your husband's caused quite a stir with his publishing affairs. King James *himself* said we are to round him up and make him give an account for the trouble he caused."

My heart thumped in my bosom, pounding out **Danger. Danger. Danger.** I couldn't speak. My mind raced with ideas of what to say, trying them one at a time to see how they might fit this situation. Nothing I could think to say seemed the right approach.

When I said nothing for, I really cannot say how long, one of them said, "I have orders here to confiscate anything related to his publishing work. We know he prepares what he prints here. In this very house."

The one with the papers added, "Would save us the trouble and you the misery of searching the whole house if you'd point out where he does his work."

I nodded my consent and pointed up the stairs to the garret where William and the others pored over manuscripts they planned to publish. I stood at the bottom of the stairs, clutching Patience's hand, frantically thinking what I should do. I knew my husband was likely to return from the university soon. He might come home at any moment. Would they take him away?

I wanted to run to the university to find him; but I could not very well leave these strangers sifting through our things. They came back down the stairs and announced, "We have here what we need. And we sealed off the room. We shall not bother you further, but your husband must know, our magistrates dare not disobey an edict from King James. If your husband is caught publishing any more blasphemy against the king's church, we shall be obliged to arrest him and return him to England."

They bid me good-bye and left. I collapsed on the steps and cried. Patience sat beside me and put her arm around my shoulders. In that instant we traded places, the child consoling the mother. "It will be well, Mother. Don't fret. Pastor Robinson will know what to do."

Dear Lord, what is to become of us now? We sat there until the bells of town hall chimed. They sounded like a summons for me to rise and figure out what to do. Leaving Patience at the house, I went to find Jonathan and implored him to find his father at the university. "Warn him not to come home. Not just yet. Then go to the Robinsons and bring the children back home."

Jonathan was a long time returning, but when he did, he told me, "Father wants you to pack a few of his things. He said you would know best what he might need. He said to be sure to include some of his books." *Naturally he would think of that. The house could be going up in fire and he would grab his books before he would leave. Of course, he would make sure all of us were out first.*

"They placed a seal on the door to his study. I dare not break it!"

"Well then, I shall go back to Robinsons and borrow a few books from Pastor Robinson. At least a Bible and the Ainsworth Psalter and a few others. Father told me to take the things you pack to Pastor Robinson. I believe he knows where Father has gone but would not tell

Kathryn Brewster Haueisen

me. I think he plans to keep Father's whereabouts from us so that should any officials return, we can truthfully say we do not know where he is."

I thanked Jonathan and hugged him until he gently pushed me away. Now a grown man, Jonathan was a steady source of strength for all of us. Bless him. He never had the opportunities his father did to prolong his studies. Once we settled in Leyden, he went straight to work making ribbons in a factory to help support us. Gratitude for his soothing presence enveloped me like a warm quilt on a chilly evening. I put a few things in a worn leather knapsack and gave it to Jonathan.

He looked so much like his father did at the same age. For the remainder of the day, I alternated between pacing and crying. I was acquainted with sorrow, but this, this disappointment after all our sacrifices getting to Leyden, seemed the deepest and darkest one of all. It was simply more than I could endure. Patience took charge of the others and prepared supper. I was too distracted to eat. The question, 'Now what shall I do?' played over and over in my mind. I was numb with worry. Only a few hours earlier the day had been so lovely. Now it was a disaster with no resolution in sight.

When all the children were fed, Patience came to sit next to me. She took my hands in hers and told me, "I know Father is safe. We may not know where he is, but I believe with my whole heart that he is safe. We will help you Mother. Fear and I are nearly grown. Jonathan already is. You have us. All will be well, and all shall be well. Is that not what Father would say if he were here?"

It was, but thinking about our circumstances made cry again. I wanted my husband here with me, but he was not. And I knew not where he was or when I would see him again. I could make a list of woes that would stretch back past Amsterdam to England.

One by one each of my children offered me what comfort they could muster. Their tenderness added to my misery. I should be comforting *them*. Accepting their ministrations made me feel inadequate at my primary purpose in life; to protect and care for my children.

Chapter 3

July 18, 1619

Reverend Robinson and Bridget came today. Their companionship eased some of the terror I have felt ever since the magistrates left with William's things. I keep imagining how upset William will be when he learns what they did to his study. I know he will understand I was powerless to prevent it. Yet, I still wonder if he will be upset with me as well. My mind races with uncertainty.

I passed the hours as if in a trance. Sleep eluded me, yet I lacked the ability to accomplish even the simplest of tasks. I dropped things. I bumped into things. I cut my thumb trying to cut up an apple. Whether I was laying down, sitting up or walking about, my mind churned with images of William. The children sat with me, bringing me food I could not swallow, asking me questions I could not answer, suggesting things I had not the strength to do. My throat constricted so that trying to swallow a piece of bread felt as though invisible hands choked me.

Patience rubbed my back. Fear held my hands. Jonathan announced he would stay with us until we knew William's fate. He opened his own worn copy of the Geneva Bible and read Deuteronomy 31:6 to us. It was a passage William read often when we faced various difficult situations. *Pluck up your hearts therefore, and be strong: dread not, nor be afraid of them: for the Lord thy God himself doth go with thee: he will not fail thee, nor forsake thee.*

As he read the familiar words, I looked out through the window watching the stars begin to twinkle in the heavens. Telling this part of our family's story, I always think back to all the nights aboard the *Mayflower* and how seeing them appear seemed so magical. Watching them that night as Jonathan's deep voice read the ancient words of encouragement carried me even further back to my girlhood days when adults soothed me, as now my children attempted to comfort me.

The night grew darker, the house grew quieter. We were talked out. The only sound came from outside where crickets chirped and cats screeched in a fight over some scrap of food. I must have slept, for I remember waking up to see sunshine streaming in. The children let Buddy spend the night inside, something I would normally never have tolerated. I suspect they thought I was so distracted I wouldn't notice. I also thought perhaps they sought comfort from the dog that I was not giving them at the moment. I found the dog dozing in a warm spot the sun created on the floor. I couldn't muster the energy to protest when Buddy woke, stretched and followed me to stir the embers to get the fire going again. He sat on his haunches and looked at me with big black eyes, inviting me to pat his head. I did, and I actually felt a little better for it.

I couldn't help but smile when I saw the look on Love's face when he saw Buddy by my side. His eyes doubled in size. I'm confident he expected a stern scolding. "Would you be so kind as to escort Buddy outside where he belongs?" By way of answer, he grabbed Buddy by the scruff of his neck and pulled him out the door. Secretly, I was grateful Love and Wrestling had Buddy. I still believed dogs belonged outside with other animals, but it seemed Buddy did help them cope with what was happening to us.

Kathryn Brewster Haueisen

When Love opened the door, Pastor Robinson and Bridget were approaching. Pastor Robinson cautiously knocked on the open door and peeked in. Love followed them back inside, closed the door to keep Buddy out, and slinked out of sight, still apparently fearing a scolding for letting the dog spend the night inside.

When Bridget saw the state of my demeanor, she rushed to embrace me. The three of us sat at the table for some time without speaking. Bridget put her hands over mine. Pastor Robinson cleared his throat several times. He would stand and walk about, then sit and stare out the window. Words seemed useless. Would they bring William back? Would they stop King James' demands?

At last Pastor Robinson spoke. "Mary, you must not fret. This is all part of God's plan for our fellowship. I believe it. We have prayed and pondered this matter over and over, considering every possible outcome. I assure you; William is safe. Even I do not know where, but I do know he is. I have friends at the university. They have friends in the city administration. They report to me he is safe. These men are trustworthy." He cleared his throat, still uneasy when looking at my desolate expression.

"Rather than see this as a tragedy, I see this as a sign. As clear as the rainbow after the flood or the miraculous way the Red Sea parted when the ancient Israelites thought they would all drown or be drawn through with Egyptian swords. This turn of events must mean the Lord is calling us to come out from Leyden to establish our own community. We will, with the help of God who leads us, we will establish a colony where we worship as the good Lord intended people to worship. We will live as a covenanted community, and all will be well."

His conviction was compelling. Bridget gently added, "You are as dear to me as my own sisters. I will help you."

Jonathan and Patience joined us. They nodded their agreement and Jonathan said, "You know we will too, Mother."

Pastor Robinson stood to leave. "You have only to believe and be strong. Be at peace, Mary. Be at peace."

I was not at peace, but I did feel less perturbed. As I concluded so often before, there was no other option. I had to be faithful and strong and at least pretend to be confident for the sake of the children. *When there is nothing I can do about a situation, the best course of action is to do nothing. I will wait and trust.*

Our fellowship continued to meet for worship and conversation about the grand plan. Months passed with occasional news that William was fine but staying out of sight. One week someone suggested he might be back in Scrooby among sympathetic family or friends there. Another week someone else reported hearing he was in London among friends introduced to him by Mr. Winslow, or people who remembered him from his years in service to Sir Davison. Yet another week someone assured me that he had been spotted in Amsterdam. Some suggested he was traveling under the name of Mr. Williamson rather than Brewster. I simply did not know, but I grew used to the way things were. This was not the whole of my life as Mrs. Brewster, only a current part of a whole life. I felt certain the situation would change.

One day Pastor Robinson asked me to accompany him to a house I had never noticed before. "This is the home of one of my colleagues at the university. He supports our plans to establish our own colony and wants to help us."

We entered and there sat William!

He was calm and composed, sipping a tankard of ale, and reading. Of course, he would occupy himself reading. He smiled at me as though it had been a matter of hours rather than months since our last encounter.

"I cannot linger long. Our Dutch friends wish me no ill will, but they dare not disregard the demands of King James. I arranged a time to meet with you to assure you I am hale and hearty. I will take leave this evening to another place, but we can meet safely here now and then, so long as my visits are short, and you keep our visits to yourself. Not even the children may know, Mary. That is imperative. Not Jonathan, or Patience, or any of them. It is too dangerous to entrust secrets to them."

Kathryn Brewster Haueisen

Our time together was brief. But it did much to lighten my heart. I said not one word about the brief meeting, but nonetheless, the children noticed something changed, especially Patience. "Mother, you appear . . . different. Happier. Less distracted."

I chided them. "You are surprised I believe what you constantly remind me? All is well and all will be well."

I rather enjoyed having this secret with William. It felt a bit like our easier days before we became parents, refugees, then exiles. If I couldn't see, hear, or touch him, at least I had our little secret to cling to for hope. That greatly encouraged me. I talked to him in my head throughout the day and prayed for his safety as I drifted off to sleep each evening.

Chapter 4

July 30, 1619

I find it peculiar how one ordinary day plants the seeds that grow into an extraordinary change of circumstances. That day started with a perfectly ordinary trip to the shops with the children. It ended with William gone away, a room in my own home sealed off by city officials and a subtle shift in thinking among Pastor Robinson, young William Bradford, Deacon Fuller and others. Until that day their talk had been centered around dreaming about establishing a place of our own in the New World. After that day the talk changed to how and when our fellowship would accomplish this. When men set a course, women are compelled to adjust the sails of their lives accordingly. I am thinking back a whole year to 1618 ... the hints of what was to come ...

I mark the day the magistrates came for William as the start of our leaving Leyden. Though, in some ways, the real source of this plan took root much earlier. Looking back, I believe it started with William's incessant talk about the New World. His decision to publish books challenging the Established Church and King James fertilized the idea. At first, I paid little heed to what transpired up in the garret, being grateful they had something to occupy them. The men shared a love of books and the ideas contained in them. I thought it a harmless pastime. I overheard enough of their conversation to grow curious about what they were doing but saw no need for concern. With a house full of children and frequent visitors, I had little time to think about what absorbed hours of their time each week. It seemed the idle talk of men who loved ideas.

Then one day not too long before William went into hiding, I went to visit my dear friend Bridget Robinson. She told me she overheard her husband and mine discussing an actual plan for removing our fellowship to the New World. "They seem certain we can establish our own colony there. That is what I heard them discussing as clearly as I speak with you now, Mary."

My heart sank like a stone in a pond. I clutched my bosom and took in a deep breath. Then another. And yet another. I hoped I heard it wrong. "Do you mean you heard them talk about doing something akin to that Jamestown colony?"

"That is what I heard."

"Do you think they seriously believe it is possible?"

"Yes, I believe they think it not only possible, but necessary."

"Why!? After all we endured to settle here, why must they talk about such a far-fetched idea?"

"It is not just our husbands, dear friend. Mr. Carver, Deacon Fuller and Mr. Bradford, even that Winslow chap that assists your husband. They all seem to think we should do this."

The walls of Bridget's home seemed to close in on me. I tried to imagine the seven of us on a ship for weeks. And what about Ann and Robert Pecke? Surely William could not consider taking seven children on such a dangerous adventure. I still had that nightmare from when we crossed from England of little Fear slipping into the sea forever. Then

Kathryn Brewster Haueisen

another thought struck me like a lightning bolt; what if he thought he would go and leave me here to fend for myself alone? I could not conjure any vision of how I should manage such a thing.

~ ~ ~

That very evening when I first found out our men were thinking like this, I skirted about the subject like a cat stalking a barn mouse. I wanted to hear this directly from my husband. I was thinking about how to broach the subject, when I dropped the ladle into the pot of stew simmering over the fire. I burnt my thumb trying to retrieve it. I pulled my hand back and then stumbled over a basket of turnips, sending them rolling across the floor. When I reached down to set the basket upright, I knocked a burning log loose from the fireplace into the open area, nearly catching my skirts on fire. Wrestling yelled, "Mama, look out!"

Finally, William looked up from his book. "Mary, what happened?"

I grabbed the fire tongs with one hand and pushed the log back in place. With my other hand I pointed to the wayward turnips. Wrestling chased the rolling turnips. Patience retrieved the ladle from the stew. I turned to my husband. "I heard the most astonishing thing today. Bridget Robinson said you and Pastor Robinson discussed establishing a new colony beyond the ocean! She must have misunderstood."

William pulled on his goatee for a long time before he spoke. He looked at me, then down at his open book, then around the room. He cleared his throat. "She did not misunderstand."

"Oh, William! What could possibly lead you to such a conclusion?"

"We have not come to this lightly. Pastor Robinson tells me that every week one among our fellowship approaches him with another concern about what is happening to us here. Some of our children speak

Dutch better than English. Children play games we do not approve. Our young men struggle to find good work. When they do, they earn only a pittance of what their Dutch friends earn."

"Yes, but dear husband, this is not new. It has been like this since we first arrived."

"That rather sums up our reasons for considering a colony of our own. We are now nearly ten years in Leyden, and we see little hope for a better future for our young people. It is true the Dutch have been charitable and gracious to us, but we believe we would thrive better in a situation of our own making."

~ ~ ~

After that day, it seemed every conversation between Pastor Robinson and William included some thought about establishing a colony. Pastor Robinson would concede life in Leyden was better than living in constant fear of arrest back in England. William would agree. "It is good, but not without problems. It is only a matter of time until King James learns I am behind the papers he so detests. Then he will send people across the North Sea to search for me. If we cross to the New World, I shall no longer care about affairs in England. Think of it, we can create our own Christian community, like that of the early Christians. We will create our own plantation upon which we all will work and share in the harvests. A true fellowship."

Pastor Robinson agreed with all those points. "If King James discovers you are behind smuggling books into England, your life will not be safe, even here, among the Dutch. Their tolerance is no match for the king's tyranny."

I had to admit, our lives as exiles had disadvantages. Being aliens, our sons could not join the guilds, which meant they were barred from the good jobs. Many were away for months, working on ships that sailed along the west coast of Europe on trade expeditions. What they learned on those voyages were things I preferred my sons not know.

On the surface, my life passed as it had for the past several years. I tended to duties at home, went to market and visited with other women from our fellowship. To a great extent I was shielded from what William, Pastor Robinson and others saw. My husband saw and heard plenty at the university where the young men he tutored from all over Europe told their gruesome tales. They kept him informed about the unrest and brutality toward non-conformists in their home countries. Pastor Robinson both taught and took courses there as well. His mind filled with all manner of new ideas. Though the men did not discuss these ideas with us women, both their eagerness to establish a new settlement and their concerns about events closer to home seeped through. I would find William sighing deeply while reading. Or I would come upon him pacing in the garden with his hands clasped behind his back and his head bowed low. Some evenings he clenched his jaws as he sucked his pipe and read some bit of news passed onto him by someone at the university.

~ ~ ~

A growing tension lurked just beneath the surface of our lives as we lived without my husband in the house. I carried on as if all were normal, but I tucked away my own secret thoughts. *The King will move on to other issues and William will return home. They will soon realize the folly of this plan. We could never pay for such a voyage. We have no aptitude for living in the wilderness. It is too dangerous, there are savages there that kill settlers.* For the time being, I said no more about the matter and concentrated on all that I needed to do to care for my children.

~ ~ ~

When William first commenced his publishing work, I was grateful for something to compensate for the responsibilities of the Manor that I knew he missed sorely. The publishing meant he spent more time at home in the garret. If I needed him, I had only to send one of the children up to fetch him for me. The publishing brought another new blessing into our lives; for that is how we became acquainted with the young English chap Edward Winslow. Mr. Edward Winslow had experience working in a London stationary shop, which proved beneficial to William's publishing efforts when Edward showed up in Leyden. He easily assimilated into our fellowship and in 1618 he married Elizabeth Barker. I especially enjoyed the days he brought his young bride with him when he came to assist William. While the men labored in the garret just months before it would be closed, Elizabeth worked with me, alongside Patience and Fear. Our many hands made light of the work that never ended.

Trouble.

Such a simple word for all that descended upon us.

Our peaceful years in exile came to an abrupt end in 1619 when King James demanded the Dutch authorities do something about the anonymous publications smuggled into England.

When we lived in England, William often confided details about his work to me on our afternoon walks. Once we went to Leyden and he set up his work in the top floor, I knew little about what he did. With William in hiding, alone in Holland was not how I pictured our lives would be when we took those long afternoon walks around Scrooby in our youth.

But then, I wonder how many people ever actually get the lives they dreamed they would have while they were growing up.

Kathryn Brewster Haueisen

Chapter 5

August 15, 1619

I depend on messages sent to me through Pastor Robinson to know where William is; though the messages never actually give me a location. I am grateful for our children who demand my attention, leaving little time to fret about all this. I suppose, if moving to the New World is indeed the Lord's plan, as Pastor Robinson seems so certain it is, I must find a way to convince myself to fully endorse it. But I still wish with all my might that this would not come to pass. As I wait to learn my fate, I think often back to former days. I am comforted with memories of when each of our children was born. I love them so much. How will this end for them? How can I protect them?

While William hid, I often let my mind wander back to the simpler days and tried to imagine what my life might have been like if I had not married William. Would I still be living in quiet northern England? My mother often said the Lord allows us to retain good memories from the past and subdues the unhappy ones so that the past appears more glamorous than it actually was. I suppose she was right. There must have been struggles I no longer remember. I wish I had been more aware of how pleasant our lives were before the troubles came upon us. Life in Scrooby Manor was always busy; it was an important regional seat where dignitaries and people of import would come for meetings or to stop on the way to and from other important gatherings. We called it the Manor, always thinking of it as a seat of power more than just our home. Most of our work dealt with postal issues and hosting important people, I never had a thought that I would ever leave the Manor; now here I am preparing my heart to leave these Dutch Lowlands for yet another place I am expected to call home.

To occupy myself while William was gone, I wrote a letter for my children that I keep tucked away in a box under our bed. If I decide to tell William about it, I shall implore him not to show it to anyone while I yet live. It shall be something for them to remember me by when I am gone. How fortunate have I been that the Lord blessed me with five children. Six actually, but that one tiny soul did not live and is buried in my heart, as well as in Leyden. When I find myself starting to wallow in self-pity, I pull out this letter and read it again, to remember my blessings. I read it often because my mind is prone to wander toward problems and away from blessings.

~ ~ ~

For my dearest Jonathan, Patience, Fear, Love & Wrestling:

This is an account of how we chose the name we gave each of you.

Jonathan, One early spring day in 1593, your father and I sat together on a stone wall around a cottage down the road from the Manor where we lived then. Our Manor wasn't just

Kathryn Brewster Haueisen

what you may think of as a big cottage. It was a very large estate and a main junction point for diplomats and other people of great importance. This is why I may be more nostalgic than you think it warrants, it was an important place and gave me a sense of importance also. At that time in 1593 I was nurturing you within my womb. It thrilled me to feel you kick and stretch. My heart skipped each time I felt you move. We discussed what to name you. I asked your father what name he proposed if you were a son. I presumed he would say William, after himself and his father before him. How like your father to veer from that which is common to follow the path set by his heart.

"I have thought much about this. A name is so important for setting the course of a child's life. What do you think about Jonathan? Was another Jonathan not the brave son of King Saul? Was he not the most loyal friend to mighty King David?"

I loved it. That is how you have come to be named Jonathan. We welcomed you with grateful hearts that August on a sweltering hot summer morning.

Patience, we chose your name for it required great patience of us as we waited for you. For six long years I thought perhaps Jonathan was to be the only child we should have. Though I longed to have another baby, month after agonizing month passed with new evidence the time had not yet come. Your dear father was so kind and patient with me. It is pitiful how cruelly some men treat a wife who does not provide him enough children quickly enough. And pity the woman who delivers only girls. I know women who have suffered humiliation and beatings when the baby was another girl. By the grace of the Lord, and my good fortune to have your father for my husband, I had no fear of retribution for my barren state. Still, I did feel peculiar going about with a lad growing so rapidly, but no other little ones with me.

Then, in the oddest way that life sometimes unfolds, my waiting was over. We were barely into the promise of a new century when we rejoiced to bring you into our little family. So, we chose for you the name that recorded what was required of us to wait for you - Patience.

Fear, though some people assume we chose your name for the circumstances of our lives surrounding the time of your birth; that is not the case at all. Our circumstances were certainly fraught with many concerns by 1605. Your father's faith led him to realize there was need for much mending in the fabric of the church. Rather than being a light unto our paths, the church had become an unwieldy burden to the very ones our dear Lord sought to comfort through it. That is how your father, along with a great many others, sought a truer path by separating from what they believed could not be purified.

The fear of the Lord compelled your father and others to defy those who were blinded by their own earthly power. How often had we heard that the fear of the Lord is the beginning of wisdom? When it came time to provide a name for you, it was natural to select Fear as a living reminder that within our own home, our lives revolved around the fear of the Lord.

I was already forty years of age when we had to bury that one precious tiny baby boy. I thought perhaps three children should be my allotment. I seldom spoke of the baby I lost, for it brought such sorrow; but I've never forgotten about **Baby William.** His tiny corpse lies buried in Leyden. His spirit lives deep within my heart. I light a small candle for him each year on his birthday. The sorrow has diminished a bit over time, as all sorrows do. Yet it is never really gone.

My dear Love, by the time the Lord blessed my womb with you, we dwelt in the pleasant city of Leyden, surrounded by friends as dear to us as our own family. The faith, hope and charity of our growing congregation made each new day a joy. Though we knew deprivations and hardships, we never lacked for care and companionship. We were as true a community of faith as ever assembled since when our Lord himself walked among the people.

What joy I felt when I again experienced the familiar signs that another baby was growing safely within my aging womb. We were so surrounded by love in our covenant community that we decided to give you a name that would capture the essence of the safe shelter we found in both the city and all the more so, within our fellowship of Separatists. We lived as did the first Christian community, singing our praises with loud shouts of exultation, so we named you Love.

My dearest Wrestling, you shall always remind us that the Lord giveth and the Lord taketh away, blessed be His name. As wonderful as our little community within our congregation had become, some grew restless and weary of the hardships living as guests in a country so different from England. There was constant talk about this strange new place across the great ocean. More than a few among our group began to dream of seeing it for themselves.

In every pub and market, people told tales of exotic brown people, rivers full of fish and beavers so large the fur of just one would make a suitable coat for a man. Father and the others within our community began to wonder if perhaps someday we might go there as well.

I thought my childbearing years were over. Then, much as the Lord surprised Sarah with a child well beyond her fertile years, I was delighted to learn we would soon add one more child to our family. I was 47 years old! I can well imagine how Sarah must have felt when at her advanced age she learned she would bear Abraham a child from her own womb. By the time you were born, our men seriously considered striking out on a grand adventure to secure our new homeland. They wrestled with the possibility of it all day and many nights. It was only natural then that we should name you Wrestling.

You have each been the joy of my life and the reason I could endure all that I faced. I urge you to love one another always, with the same tenderness I have held for you. Should I die before your father, surround him with that same gentle mercy with which you gave me through our years of turmoil and trouble.

Your loving Mother.

Kathryn Brewster Haueisen

Chapter 6

August 25, 1619

I miss William so much; I find myself wondering if I will have to spend the rest of my life settling for an occasional report about him between our short visits. I find it helps to go back in time, filling my mind with memories of when life was simple and safe. I cannot bear to think of the consequences of moving so far away. I feel torn in two. Part of me wants to cling to our life here in Leyden and fight to convince William we must not leave. Another part of me wants to be faithful to William, trusting him to know what is best for all of us, even if that means I will eventually have to leave this home. Somehow revisiting the past gives me courage for the facing of these present days.

Fear: Mother didn't speak much of the preparations for the voyage. That part of her life was full of fear and uncertainty for her. She tried to never burden us during those days, ones she referred to as her darkest period. So, all I have are the following diary entries ….

October 3, 1619

I saw William again yesterday. He looks healthy enough. He says many are sympathetic to the cause and see to it he has safe places to sleep. He says the negotiations for finding a way to transport our fellowship to the New World are coming along well. I tried to be pleased with that news, but I feel like I have rocks in my stomach. I walk about each day with a pending sense of doom.

October 15, 1619

And still William hides, I know not where. The occasional notes he smuggles to me, along with the even less frequent opportunities I have to see him for myself, provide me too much time to conjure all sorts of distasteful scenes in my head. The men report they think they have found investors in London who will finance a voyage, in exchange for our labor as indentured servants for seven years. They think this good news. I find it appalling. Once upon a time I was mistress of a grand manor in a quiet village. Now I am essentially a widow with five children expected to sign on to be a servant to men I have never met.

Kathryn Brewster Haueisen

October 21, 1619

Mr. Winslow called on us yesterday. He said he had heard from sources he trusts implicitly that William is in London this month, working as a silent partner on negotiations with a group of investors. He is silent in public, for he is hiding with friends introduced to him by Mr. Winslow. However, Mr. Winslow tells me I should be proud of him as he uses his brief diplomatic work with Sir Davison to good advantage in proposing plans for how to solicit the funding our fellowship needs. These investors call themselves the Merchant Adventurers and are eager to invest a bit of their wealth in establishing another English colony in the New World. I am relieved to know my husband is still alive and being cautious. I am also peeved that he continues to stay away when I need him here at home. Images of his arrest in England and his time in jail in Boston in 1607 fill me with dread that it might happen again.

I hardly remember the long walk back to Scrooby with the others after the ship master betrayed us for few pounds for his deceit.

October 28, 1619

The people in the fellowship outdo themselves offering help in all manner of ways. Some bring food. Some come to take the children away for a few hours so that I have time to gather my wits. We are often invited to join a family from the fellowship for a meal. Their kindness touches me deeply. Yet none of it eases my worries about where William might be and what dangers he tempts with his actions. I am propelled right back to the time he was jailed in the Boston Guildhouse. Thank the good Lord they didn't jail Jonathan. He was such a help with Patience and Fear as we trudged the miles with the other women and their children. I never thought we should endure another time of separation. I understand why our fellowship has decided to separate from the Established Church. I do not understand why that means William must separate from me.

Kathryn Brewster Haueisen

November 6, 1619

When William returned to Scrooby after being jailed in Boston he came into the room we shared in Lucinda's home with a big grin on his face and a wrapped package in his hands. The package turned out to be this diary in which I write these memories. "I thought you might put this to good use," he said as he watched me unwrap the package. I understood that was his way of expressing his regret that his decisions had resulted in me having to guide the children without his help for the days we were separated. I am grateful and the diary has helped me endure the many other challenges that have followed us since the spring of 1608 when the men decided we must leave – again. And of course the women had no say about it but prepared for another long journey with a precarious destination.

November 12, 1619

Yesterday Pastor Robinson and Bridget sat with me for a long time. I suppose he sensed my frustration, mingled with despair and even anger, at the situation I was in – again.

William stays away month after month. The Dutch are kind enough, but unable to help our situation.

Though he never apologized for the situation in which I find myself, he did offer to assist me many times in the course of the day. Finally, he offered to stay with the children, all of them, mine and his, so that Bridget and I could go to market without children. We must have walked several miles talking and stopping often to rest. We made the most of this precious time without the children.

In the midst of my troubles, I am reminded often of the kindness of friends and even strangers.

November 18, 1619

Winter has set in. Mr. Carver reports he heard William was seen with some of the Ancient Brethren fellowship in Amsterdam. It is maddening to be hearing about my husband without actually hearing from him. I inquired of Pastor Robinson when I might expect to visit him again and he said he really could not say.

More waiting.

Thank the Lord for Bridget who is my constant companion on this lonesome vigil.

November 22, 1619

The snow is flying. It is lovely and I am content to be in the house with my spinning wheel and a good fire. The canals are starting to freeze. Perhaps we shall again be able to walk on them. The children love to walk on the ice. I do not so much, as I am not as agile as they are, but I love watching them. I never thought I would learn to pull a sled over ice in canals, but it does make shopping amusing. I wonder if William is safe. I wonder where he is. It is past time for a visit.

December 2, 1619

Yesterday Pastor Robinson took me to a new home where William was waiting to greet me. We had a whole afternoon to visit. The woman who lived there is married to one of the professors at the university. He told her we would be borrowing their home for a few hours and why we needed to do so. She brought us a platter of cheese, wonderful dark rye bread, and a large pitcher of ale. Then she left, closed the door, and we tried to catch up on all that happened since we last saw each other. The time flew. I talked about the children, especially Love and Wrestling, and the dog Buddy that followed them everywhere. William talked about the plans unfolding to work out a plan with the Merchant Adventurers to finance our voyage. He is so excited about the progress. I tried to be excited with him, but I just am not.

All I see is trouble and challenges.

All he sees is opportunity and excitement.

I suppose the reality is somewhere between and betwixt. At least we were face to face for a few hours. We even laughed at some of the stories I had to tell him about Love and Wrestling.

Kathryn Brewster Haueisen

January 5, 1620

It has been over a month since I last saw William. Mr. Bradford tells me the negotiations for our voyage are coming along nicely. Those in the fellowship who have some finances have agreed to donate them to the cost of the voyage. Others have eagerly agreed to sign on as indentured servants.

The length of service to the Adventurers shall be seven years. We shall work for these investors six days a week, producing what we are able to pay off our indebtedness to them. One day a week shall be ours. And there is the rub. We require one day a week to honor the Sabbath. This requires us to set aside work and spend the day in worship and study. So that leaves us no days to establish our own financial security.

I don't see how this plan will work to our advantage. But Mr. Bradford, and many more like him, seem to think this is all good and proper. I confess that I do not understand their enthusiasm for such a plan; but there have been many things I have not understood since we arrived in Leyden.

10 January, 1620

The weather is bitterly cold. Buddy makes such a pitiful noise that I have relented and let him sleep by the fire at night. While I am never afraid here in Leyden as I often was those last years in England, it is a comfort to know Buddy would alert me should there be any more trouble from the magistrates, especially in the dark of the night. I enjoy seeing how much the boys enjoy Buddy. I can hardly believe how fast my sons have grown.

It seems only a few months ago they were babies, when in reality it has been nine years for Love and six for Wrestling.

January 12, 1620

Today I received a letter from William. It included the route it took to get to me. He gave it to Mr. Cushman who remains in London making arrangements for us to sail next summer. Mr. Cushman gave it to Mr. Winslow who was visiting some of his friends and family but planning to return soon to Leyden. Upon his arrival he was to give it to Mr. Bradford, who in turn would bring to me. He did so about mid-day.

William reports he had opportunity to visit with Mr. Davison's children and that they fare well enough. They miss their father, naturally, but they have managed to secure adequate work even though some people still think their father was a traitor. William wrote that he assured them their father was most certainly not a traitor, but rather one of the finest men he ever knew. He told me he took the time one evening to tell them how well their father served as Secretary of State to the queen. His commitment to serve her honorably was betrayed, landing him in an impossible situation; but history would surely turn a kind eye toward Sir Davison.

I added his letter to the few others he has sent me since going into hiding. And I wait and wonder when he shall no longer have to arrange secret meetings and send me letters. What will history say of us? I fear that history won't know us at all, that we will be lost at sea and only God will remember our souls.

These days of waiting weigh upon me but I must pretend to be of good cheer for the sake of the children.

January 15, 1620

For just one day I should like to go about my affairs without engaging in a conversation about the New World!

Such talk is everywhere; in our house when the children speculate when they will see their father again, at fellowship when someone always asks me what I've heard from or about William, and in our meetings when someone gives us the latest news about the negotiations for our migration across the sea. Pastor Robinson reported that the Virginia Company seems inclined to grant us a patent to establish ourselves in the New World within their claimed territory, except we need King James's approval. Pastor Robinson seems to believe His Majesty will do so. I cannot fathom why he should after he has sent his men chasing over two countries in search of William. I don't know if I should hope or pray; or how I should hope and pray.

If the king approves our request, we will be leaving here this summer. If the king does not approve the request, William remains in constant danger of arrest and execution.

Kathryn Brewster Haueisen

February 1, 1620

Six months have come and gone since the day the magistrates came. I marvel that I can still get up and tend to all that is needed to run this busy household. Though, it has become much quieter with William gone. No more university students come by. The upstairs remains sealed off and no men come and go to work on whatever they worked on up there. The only people from the fellowship who call come to offer help and consolation to me. They do not discuss much of fellowship affairs with me, being only a woman. How much longer will this go on?!

The men don't see the folly of their plan. Instead, they increase their actions toward getting the backing of the Virginia Company and permission from King James.

Pastor Robinson keeps me informed. Deacon Cushman and Deacon Carver met with William in one place or another to craft the official request for permission in such a way as to assure the king ours should be a proper religious colony, without actually promising to adhere to any offensive practices which we deplored.

Chapter 7

Fear: I have more details to offer at this part of the story. Mother was willing to talk about the last few months getting ready to sail, when the decision was finally accepted and our family was under contract with the Adventurers. Being younger than my sister Patience, I don't recall much of those final months when Father was gone, but we were all with Mother. I do remember the nasty conflict between Mother and Patience about why they decided to leave us and Jonathan behind but were taking Love and Wrestling. So, I again share this story from the stories Mother told me when we were finally reunited. I loved her stories, so I remember all the details very well. Mother told me . . .

~ ~ ~

Pastor Robinson gathered our fellowship to discuss how migration to the New World might become reality. Several among our fellowship had spent over a year soliciting financial support, traveling back and forth to London to petition men they knew had the means, if not yet the will, to fund our voyage. Mr. Carver and Mr. Cushman accomplished a great deal, but for all their efforts we didn't have sufficient finances to take all of us; by then we were a fellowship of over three hundred. We would need several ships to take that many, along with everything we would need to start a new settlement. We would be totally on our own, so vast supplies were a necessity. Secretly, I was relieved. *Good enough, let others go across the ocean and report back what they find and how they fare.*

I sat with the women and children, listening as one man after another set forth his proposals for how we should proceed. Eventually, they agreed only a small group would go now on two ships that would deliver our people and supplies. One ship would return and the other would stay in the New World, enabling the settlers to explore the area and perhaps establish a fishing business to help repay the investors.

Mr. Carver was able to pay his own passage, and willingly offered his resources to help others. Some quickly agreed to enter into indentured servant arrangements to get us started. It seemed to be coming together.

I felt calm enough about the plan until Pastor Robinson spoke these terrible words. "Given we can only send a small number of our fellowship now, perhaps forty or so, I must stay here and care for the others, until such a time as we can all be reunited. I have given great thought to the matter. I believe Elder Brewster should go with you as your spiritual leader until I can join you. I have communicated this to him, and he has agreed he is willing to do so."

I nearly fainted. *No! He cannot cross the ocean and leave us here! But it would simply be impossible to move our family so far, under such mean circumstances. No!*

I was alone in my response. Others heartily agreed to the plan, "Here, here," responses erupted throughout the fellowship. What Mr. Carver said next restored a glimmer of hope. "We are agreed then. We have only a few matters left. We must select the others who will go first. And we must wait to confirm that the Virginia Company has granted us our charter to establish our colony at the mouth of the Hudson River. And that our negotiators have convinced King James to let us do so. The Virginia Company will fund such a charter. Of that, I am certain."

I relaxed a bit. I could not see how they expected to procure a charter when we lived in exile away from England and the Virginia Company. But then, I had little knowledge of all the negotiations

Kathryn Brewster Haueisen

transpiring between Mr. Carver and Mr. Cushman and the powerful London businessmen. They seemed certain that the Virginia Company would gladly pay for our voyage if they believed it would benefit them. Mr. Cushman reiterated, "Using our labor, they intend to establish a lucrative trade business in the New World. We have only to work for them for a few years and we shall be free of both the English enforcers and the Dutch lax society."

How naïve I was.

I believed the plan would fail and our lives would continue on as the past twelve years.

~ ~ ~

The meeting concluded but I stayed seated. I instructed Patience and Fear to take the younger children to the house. I wanted to be alone with my thoughts. I was fuming that William so willingly agreed to put our family through such turmoil and to allow me to learn about it in a public meeting. I was also frightened. William was again in danger. If the authorities found him, they'd surely send him back to England to be tried and . . . I forced my mind not to finish the thought. *What an impossible predicament. Leaving is too great a price to pay. Staying is too great a risk to take. When I committed to for better or for worse, I was thinking about sickness and poverty; not anything like this!*

Pastor Robinson and Bridget waited until all the others left. They sent their own children upstairs. Together they approached and sat on a bench facing me. Pastor Robinson did look sorry as he said, "I regret this is how you learned of this, Mary. I tried to find another way, a better way, but I could not. William has been away in England, working out of sight with Mr. Carver and Mr. Cushman to make our arrangements. He wanted to tell you himself, but there were delays in his travel arrangements. He will be back in Leyden before the week passes. I will arrange for you to see him."

When next I saw William, well the day was tumultuous. I had never before openly challenged any decision William made after he explained it to me and told me his reasons. I might not like his conclusions, but I did trust him to always act on what he was convinced was the right path. When I had my chance to see him again, I unleashed all the fears, frustrations and fury I'd been harboring for months. Though the walls in the room where we had our secret meeting had thick stones, I would not be surprised to learn others heard my burst of anger.

All these years later, I cannot recall my exact words, but I can still feel the waves of emotion that washed over me and spewed out like an angry river after a heavy rain. William stood statue still as I spit out one accusation after another. "And the children! William, have you considered the children? How am I to manage seven children in the wilderness?"

When I finished, he said nothing at first. He stroked his goatee and gestured that we should sit down. We sat. I waited. Eventually he spoke. "I count you my dearest treasure on this troubled earth. I regret the worry I have caused you. Yet, I must do as I believe the good Lord directs me. I believe with all my heart, and mind, and soul, that we are called to take this path across the water, to a new land. Just as Abraham was called to leave Ur. And Moses was called to lead the people out of Egypt."

"That was all fine and good for them, but they did not worry about the children, now, did they? They left that to the women. And this woman is not up to this." I raised my apron to wipe first my eyes and then my nose.

"Yes. Of course, you speak rightly. And that is why we shall take only Love and William."

"What?"

Thus, the afternoon passed. William revealed one detail at a time. I protested point by point. In the end the matter was decided. He, I, and the younger boys would be among the first group to go. The Pecke children were old enough to go into other households as

Kathryn Brewster Haueisen

apprentices. Jonathan was already an adult with his own home. Patience and Fear would stay with the Robinsons.

There I was again, in a situation where my only realistic option was to comply with the wishes and decisions of my husband.

Since it was my only option, I would comply.

But I didn't have to like it.

Chapter 8

June 20, 1620

I saw William again yesterday. Rather than feeling calmer for it, I feel more irritated and discouraged than ever. He insists we shall take only the younger boys with us. The others will stay with the fellowship and join us when they can. I do not know if I can bear this; but I see no way around it. The fellowship wants him to go in place of Pastor Robinson. He wants to secure our daughters' safety by leaving them here with Jonathan and the rest of the community. Now I understand why Rachel wept for her children and could not be consoled. We have not left yet and already I feel a hole in my soul where my daughters and Jonathan belong.

I had a horrible row with Patience a few days after I met with William in secret. Of course, I understood she is an adult. I was already engaged to William when I was her age. That is precisely why she could not, she must not, go with us. I had hoped by now she would be settled with a husband in her own home. Since she was not, I reluctantly agreed with William that it was best she stay in Leyden. There certainly would not be a suitable husband in the wilderness.

"Mother, you must convince Father to allow me to come with you. I will help with Love and Wrestling."

"Your Father has made up his mind and no one can convince him to change course once he has determined what to do. You must stay here."

"I don't want to stay here, perhaps to never see you again. Do you not care about what happens to me?"

I reached to sooth her hair as had been my custom for nigh on twenty years. She pulled away, crossed her arms, and sat down with a thud on a chair.

"Patience, dear, if only you could imagine how my heart is shattering at the very thought of leaving you here. But I must agree with your father, this is truly the best course for all of us. You should soon be marrying and where would you find a husband in the New World?"

"Oh, Mother! I am not ready to marry. Other women my age are going. Dorothy Bradford is going."

"Dorothy goes with her husband, as you well know. Even she is leaving her son John here with her parents. I do not profess to know much about this new place, but the stories I have heard make it sound equally wonderful and treacherous. I cannot risk taking two unwed young women into the untamed wilderness. There may be wild beasts that would attack you. If they do not, then maybe the Indians would. No, Patience. You must stay here, to look over Fear and to help Jonathan. He still grieves the deaths of his wife and child."

Patience bit her lip and twirled a strand of hair around her finger. "This is not right."

I sat down beside her. I agreed. None of this seemed right to me. Yet William and the others were determined this was the way it ought to be. How I wanted William to be the one having this conversation with Patience. Where was he? A good question that had no answer I could latch onto. Hiding somewhere. I got messages about his whereabouts from time to time. Yet for months on end, the work of preparing to leave fell to me.

"Mother, you need me to help you. My place is with you, and Love and Wrestling."

How hard it is to argue in favor of a thing I so much wanted to argue against. I agreed with Patience. I wanted her, and Fear, and also Jonathan, with me. But William had made up his mind. How could I fight his logic? I could not.

And that was that.

So now, here I was, upsetting my daughter, foisting upon her a decision neither of us would ever choose. I so wanted to hurt him by laying all the blame on him so that his children would be angry with him. Yet I knew my duty was to ease the blame from his shoulders so that he could carry on his work. Not only duty, but despite my anger, I still loved my husband, and his relationship with his children was worth more than my releasing my feelings right now.

~ ~ ~

I wanted my last afternoon with my dear friend Bridget to be a happy one. I took Love and Wrestling with me, along with more things for Patience and Fear and went to the Robinsons. I was overcome with gratefulness that Bridget would watch over Patience and Fear, but equally distraught that they needed a new home.

Love and Wrestling entered the Robinson's home ahead of me and bounded up the stairs. I had to stop midway to catch my breath, and also to collect my thoughts and prepare myself for this final private visit together. I dreaded saying farewell to her.

Bridget set things straight at the start. "Love, Wrestling, come look at what I have for you." The boys dashed over to where she stood at the table. She pulled out two large balls of yarn, one blue and one red.

"I've fixed these so they will not unravel. You can use them as balls to play with as you make your way to your new home."

She sounded so calm, as if we were merely moving down the street and not across the world. To manage the squabble that often ensues when the boys have to select something, she lured them into a game. With both hands behind her back, she said, "I hold a small piece of yarn in my hand. Whichever of you guesses both the color and which hand I have it in, will be the first to select the ball you want."

Wrestling jumped up and down with glee when he guessed correctly and chose the blue ball. The boys sat down and began rolling their balls back and forth, trying to make them collide.

"Please, do not talk of the trip," I begged. "Let us pretend this is like any other afternoon when we pass the time in one another's company."

"I agree that is the best plan, but I do have something for you, so you will not forget me."

"I will never, ever forget you."

Bridget left and quickly returned with a locket on a delicate chain. "My father gave this to my mother many years ago. I have treasured it, and now I want you to have it."

My throat grew thick, my tongue seemed stuck and incapable of moving. I reached out to touch it. "I don't think I should accept a treasure that belongs to your family," I finally managed to say.

"*That* is precisely why I want you to have it. You have been as family to me. And now your daughters live with me as though they were my own kin. Please accept this."

She took my hand and pressed the locket into my palm, curling my fingers around it. I put my clenched fist against my breast and murmured, "Thank you. I will treasure it always."

On the way home I walked slowly, trying to press the image of every shop I passed deep into my mind. I stood along the canal remembering the day I first saw this place and how we all gasped at the beauty of the city.

Kathryn Brewster Haueisen

Then a shadow of dread encircled me as I thought about how soon I would see this place for the last time. The weight of the realization hurt with a physical pain. This was the place where both these boys were born, the only place they knew. I wanted to stay by the canal longer, but my sons commenced arguing and my attention was diverted.

When we turned the corner, I sent them ahead to our house. "Go straight into the house. Wait for me there. I shall not be long." They protested, but I think the tone of my voice convinced them to do as I bid.

Once I could see them inside the gate to our garden, I turned the other way and walked the short distance to the back of Pieterskerk. I debated if I should go around to the front and say my prayers inside the sanctuary or if I ought to remain outside, closer to the house, and trust the Lord would hear my petitions equally well from outside the church.

I opted to stay outside.

It was a sunny late afternoon with a breeze to keep me cool and comfortable. I paced a bit, trying to quiet my thoughts and ponder what precisely I wished to ask of the Lord. In the end I settled for repeating our Lord's own prayer several times and adding a simple plea for the courage to do what must be done and forgiveness for not wanting to do it.

When I entered the house, I found Wrestling and Love jostling one another and Fear trying to stop them. In my vexation I raised my voice, which caught their attention at least. "Love! Wresting! I have neither time nor patience for this! You must mind me, and in my absence, you must mind your sisters or your brother or any other adult. Do you understand?"

Since they rarely heard me speak so firmly, they stopped and stared at me. I repeated, "Do. . . you. . . understand. . . me?" I scowled and waited for a response.

Hearing none, I demanded, "Answer me when I speak to you!"

Both jumped to their feet. Love meekly looked up. "Yes, Mother." He then nudged Wrestling in the ribs and Wrestling mumbled, "Yes."

I didn't know what to do next. I thanked Fear for trying to corral her brothers and chased the boys out into the garden. I stirred the logs in the fireplace. I paced. I wanted to cry, but I also wanted to appear calm and confident. It was my place to help William execute this plan, even in his absence. Especially in his absence.

My hopes that praying before preparing for our departure would sooth me were dashed. I was more agitated than before I paused at Pieterskerk. I believed, truly I did. The whole of the Apostle's Creed we recited every Sunday. The Lord's Prayer. I believed it all, but I so wanted to release my confusion, fears, and frustrations at the Lord. I sorely wanted to, but dared not. Once we left tomorrow, I would no longer have Bridget, or even Jonathan and my daughters. I didn't know when I would see William again. I would be truly on my own and how would I manage if I stirred the wrath of God?

~ ~ ~

I don't know how I survived that last evening. When I stopped pacing to sit for a few moments to determine what to do next, Fear approached. "Here, Mother. While you were gone Mrs. Carver came by with this note. She said her husband got it from Mr. Cushman who got it from someone who got it from Father."

How like William. Though he believed he best protected me and our children by staying hidden away, he managed to send me a message. He must have guessed how desperately I wanted to hear from him at this time. Unable to come himself, he sent a note through a chain of friends. The note contained a little of Psalm 145, *The Lord is gracious, full of compassion, slow to anger, and of great mercy. The Lord is good to all, and his tender mercies are over his works.* The psalm melody from the

Ainsworth Psalter ran through my mind and I began to hum it. When I read his signature, my frustration and consternation with him evaporated. *With all my love and gratitude and affection for being my Ebenezer.*

The rest of the message was so typical William, I chuckled to myself. He sent instructions to me regarding which of his books I should pack to bring along. *Be sure to include the **Book of Martyrs**,* he wrote. *That will remind me why we do this should my determination decline.*

Unlike when we hurried out of England like common thieves, taking only what we could carry, I had a large trunk and additional bags in which to take what we might need; which was essentially everything we needed to live for years to come. As I packed our things my mind filled with image after image of what the New World could be like. I was sure it did not include cobble streets, canals and markets.

William's note further instructed me to give the rest of his books to Pastor Robinson, along with a note for him. His note to Pastor Robinson read: *Perhaps you will be so kind as to save these books for me until such a time as you can bring them to me yourself or make arrangements for one of our members to deliver them in the future. With great fondness, your friend, William Brewster.*

Grateful to have a task to do, I set about sorting through William's many books, totaling near a hundred. I sometimes wondered if he loved them more than his family. I never asked, perhaps because I feared hearing the answer.

With the books sorted, I set out our supper of turnips, carrots and peas for the children. Patience and Fear picked at their suppers in stony silence. We had said to one another all we needed to say. More words would not ease the pain of parting. I feared should I try to put words to the apprehension swirling about within me like leaves blown off the tree in a storm, I would cry. If I yielded to tears, that would surely start an avalanche of more tears from others. No, this was a time to shove the pain way, way down. I could retrieve it later. For now, I must focus on things minute by minute. Supper seemed to take a day, but also passed in a blink of the eye.

Jonathan dropped by to see if I needed his assistance, breaking the spell of silence.

"What I need from you this evening is to stay with your brothers while I go with your sisters to take over a few more things they will need when we . . . " I couldn't bring myself to say it. "That is, you know, when . . ." He took three long strides toward me and put his arms around me.

"I will take care of Love and Wrestling tonight. And all will be well. All shall be well. Father told me that when he parted from me. I believe him. Go now and see for yourself how the Robinsons have prepared a place for Fear and Patience. Just as Jesus prepared a place for his disciples on that last night with them. Be at peace, Mother. All shall be well."

His tenderness did comfort me. In part because his words sounded so much like those his father often said. Even the voice sounded almost exactly like William's deep, clear voice. It pleased me to see what an intelligent, caring and capable young man he truly had become.

Patience, Fear, and I walked along the canal. The moon's reflection shimmered in the ripples of the canal water. The night was warm, even for July, with a slight breeze that felt refreshing on my face. There was nothing more to say, so we walked arm and arm in silence.

Pastor Robinson greeted us when we knocked. If he was surprised to have us at his doorstep at the last streaks of daylight, he showed it not in his demeanor.

"Welcome, welcome. Do come in. Patience, Fear, after this evening, you need not knock before you enter. You are part of our family now. Come, let me show you where you can put your things."

He settled the girls and insisted on escorting me back home, to the place that, after this night, would never be my home again.

Kathryn Brewster Haueisen

"Mary, I am glad you came with the girls. I have rehearsed again and again what I would like to tell you but thought I might never have the chance to speak the words I practiced."

I was taken aback. *What more is there to say?*

He continued as we strolled slowly. "I feel some obligation to you to try to explain, as I know William often must have done. This way of life, our total commitment to our Lord, to what we believe the Lord compels us to do, it can be a burden. I know William feels it too. The weight of being responsible to you—and your wonderful children—it is a heavy burden. I do not mean imply that *you* are a burden. No, never that."

I waited for him to go on, trying to fathom what he was trying to say. He fumbled his words as a young man about to propose marriage might do.

"What I mean to say is that, sometimes, in the course of a man's life, he has to do less than he would like in one area of his life, in order to do more in another." He stopped; I think anticipating I would say something to indicate I understood. But I did not yet understand, so I remained silent.

"William loves you very much. I hear it in his tone whenever he speaks your name. That is most certainly true. Yet he is equally compelled to follow as he believes the Lord directs. He is often in anguish struggling to discern how to sort out his loyalty to his Lord over against his obligation to provide for you and the children. He is certain, as am I, that this chance to establish our own colony in the New World is what we are meant to do. Mary, he is worried about how this will affect you, yet he sees no other course but to proceed with our plans."

I already knew this. Had I not tried to dissuade him? Had I not offered to stay behind with the children? I reminded him, "I did offer to stay, secure in the assurance you and Bridget would assist me. He would not hear of it."

"Yes, I know. We discussed the advantages and disadvantages of that often. In the end, I believe he simply did not think he could go without you. I prevailed upon him to lead our people in their daily prayers and reflections on God's word until I join you. We cannot all go at once. We struggled to secure what funding we do have. Our people will perish without the milk of the Holy Scriptures to sustain them. We concluded he would go along with this first group and I and the others will stay here, working and saving and looking to secure future funding."

I heard this premise more times than I could recall, and again had nothing to say. He stopped walking and turned to me with a such a pitiful look. This man who could preach and teach for hours on end seemed totally void of words for this situation.

"What I urge you to do, what I fervently hope you will do, is to trust William and be his Ebenezer when he needs you. For he *will* need you. Though he speaks with confidence and assurance, I am his confessor. I know how it torments him to think of how you grieve so about leaving Patience and Fear in our care. And Jonathan as well, though he is quite a capable young man himself.

"I pledge to you, my dear sister in Christ, that your son and daughters will want for nothing. I know you will miss them, and they you. Yet, I also know we are all bound together with chords that cannot be broken. Our mutual affection and love for one another and for our Lord weaves us together as family as surely as so many among us have learned to weave on looms here in Leyden.

"Tomorrow, we must bid each other farewell for now, and endure the miles that separate us, but we will always carry each other here." He tapped his chest. "And here." He pointed to his forehead. "And here." He covered his stomach with both hands. "For it is true that God has joined us together, and neither man nor oceans can ever sever us from one another."

By the time he managed to say what he had rehearsed, we arrived back at my home. A home filled so often with laughter and tears. The home where I fed university students William brought home, along with young single adults and his publishing colleagues. The home where Love and Wrestling took their first breaths and the Pecke children found shelter when orphaned.

I resolved I would not allow myself to dwell on all I had to leave behind.

"I bid you good evening, dear friend. I will honor your request in every way within my power. We will gather with you tomorrow for a service together. Thank you for seeing me home."

Chapter 9

July 20, 1620

> *My heart and mind overflow with so many thoughts. The paths taken that have led me to the eve before I must leave this place I have come to love. Sorrow threatens to consume me. The tender words Pastor Robinson spoke to me just now. How he affirms how much William looks to me for strength. It is true, William does treat me more as his equal than most men I know do their wives. I pray I will have the strength to endure tomorrow.*

The following morning, July 21, 1620, the fellowship gathered to worship at the Robinson's home. Pastor Robinson asked everyone to find a seat. Jonathan guided Love and Wrestling to the men's side. Patience and Fear sat on either side of me on the women's side.

I could smell the aroma of something good coming from the open stairway leading up to the Robinson quarters. We gradually quieted ourselves and he began. "This is the day the Lord has made and we will rejoice in it." I most certainly did not feel like rejoicing. Whatever the exact opposite of rejoicing would be, that is how I felt.

Perhaps I only imagined it, but I thought he emphasized *will* a bit more than usual. "Mrs. Robinson and some of others are at work upstairs preparing a meal for us. As this will be the last time we fellowship together until we are all safely relocated to our new colony, I told them they could miss the start of our service." Women generally had only one reason for being absent from worship: that was giving birth to a baby. Today they had a second: preparing the last supper for those of us departing from all that was familiar to venture into the wilderness.

His announcement confirmed it. Our situation was both solemn and irreversible. "And of course dear Elder Brewster is not with us. He has gone across to England to assist Mr. Carver and Mr. Cushman with final details for the voyage. For his safety, and ultimately also ours as well, he remains in hiding. Even I do not know where he is, other than somewhere in London. He plans to board the *Mayflower* in Southampton as Mr. Williamson."

This news gave me a minuscule measure of comfort. At least he had made it safely across to England again. I trusted Mr. Carver and Mr. Cushman to do all within their power to protect him.

"I have received late and, I fear, rather unwelcome news. But even in this blow, I see the hand of God at work. Our investors have insisted you must travel with a group of men and women who are not part of our fellowship."

Audible bursts of "What?" and "No" and "They cannot do that!" erupted.

Ignoring them all, he continued, "It seems in their eagerness to assure a profit from this venture, they have sold spaces on the ships to some who long to explore the New World but care not to work as indentured servants to do so. They were quite firm on this point."

More exasperated cries arose. Mr. Bradford was on his feet demanding, "What right have they do to this! We paid good money for

Kathryn Brewster Haueisen

the passage and many of us have pledged our labor for seven long years for them. Is that not enough?"

Pastor Robinson waved his hands to indicate we should all resume our seats.

"It is not what we wanted; but it is what we must endure, or they shall refuse us any further assistance. Even in this last-minute bit of trickery, there is already some good. Captain Myles Standish is among those assigned to travel with you. He shall defend you from all danger. He served admirably among the English troops when we were in Amsterdam. Remember how we often saw English soldiers here in the low country? I have heard he is even now packing weapons and ammunition for the trip. He has ample experience to serve you well."

Crossed arms and scowling faces communicated that Pastor Robinson's efforts to placate us fell short of the mark. He stepped back a few paces. "There is yet more news. Mr. Carver and Mr. Cushman were also told that four abandoned children must also sail with you."

"No!" protested Deacon Samuel Fuller, jumping to his feet.

Pastor Robinson continued as though he had not spoken. "They are four of God's precious children, in urgent need of someone to care for them. They will travel as servants. Ellen is eight, Jasper is seven, Richard six and Mary is but four. I have already discussed the matter with Mr. Carver and Mr. Cushman. They have conferred with Elder Brewster." He reached into his vest and pulled out a letter and read it to us:

Thomas Weston now has in his care four children who are without parents to properly provide for them. He has determined that they should travel with the others to the New World. They are to be sufficiently kept and maintained with meat, drink, apparel and lodging. At the end of seven years, they shall have 50 acres of land apiece in Virginia.

Pastor Robinson folded the letter and tucked it back inside his vest. "As I am sure you know, Mr. Weston is one of our investors, one of the leaders of the Adventurers actually. Have we truly any choice in the matter? Aside from being the Christian response required of us, it is also imperative that we not cross Mr. Weston. In correspondence with Elder Brewster, we have assigned Richard and Ellen More to the Elder's family." He paused to look at me and smile.

Did he know this last night? He must have known it then! I felt betrayed. Smooth-talked into going along with the grand plan when he must have known he would be announcing this now. I could feel my checks grow hot and bile inch up in my stomach. I did not return his smile. Why had he not told me this last night? Was he afraid I would refuse? As if I had any more say in this matter than I had in any other aspect of this. Servants, indeed. Two more children needing constant supervision more likely. Well, add them to the list of chores requiring my attention. We leave the Pecke children with the fellowship and before I even gave them a proper farewell, I have two more to take their place. In my bitterness I figured something would happen and the other two would eventually also be assigned to my care.

Pastor Robinson hurried to announce that Jasper would travel with the Carver family and little Mary would go with the Winslow family. With all the disconcerting announcements handled, he transformed his demeanor from solemn to energized. As was his weekly custom, he was ready with an encouraging word. He urged us to join with other godly ministers who may arrive in the New World. He stressed that we must always endeavor to seek unity in the Christian church rather than division. "Be ready to receive whatever further truth God might reveal, for it is not possible the Christian world should come so lately out of such thick anti-christian darkness, and that the full perfection of knowledge should break forth at once."

His admonishment perhaps sprang from challenges we experienced when we first arrived in Amsterdam. I had nearly forgotten how contentious life was among some of the earlier English exiles. "We are Separatists, true enough. But foremost we are Christians and must

Kathryn Brewster Haueisen

strive to act as such at all times and in every way. We must set an example by conducting ourselves as such. I have spent many hours advising Elder Brewster what he must know to provide you proper spiritual nourishment and care."

I looked over to see Mr. Winslow and Mr. Bradford diligently writing down these words of instruction, I presume to share with William when we were reunited, and perhaps also for instruction to the children as they grew to an age of understanding.

Shortly after the service ended, the women who had been laboring upstairs appeared with platters and baskets full of delicious smelling dishes. Bridget carried a large platter of roasted goose, sprinkled generously with ground turmeric root. The aroma sent my stomach into spasms of hunger pangs. Her sister, Katherine Carver, was right behind her with another large platter of goat cheese.

"It is a feast fit for a king!" declared Mr. Winslow when his wife Elizabeth passed by with a plate of beautifully arranged sliced apples and oranges, surrounded with clusters of large red grapes. Soon the table at the back of our worship area was laden with the many marvelous dishes the women had lovingly prepared. A parade of children went up and the down the stairs, bringing down what their mothers and grandmothers entrusted them to add to the table.

I wiped away tears watching it all transpire. I noticed I was not the only one overcome by the kindness and generosity of these dear people. I felt a stab of sorrow as clearly as if someone had come at me with a knife thinking about how this would be our last fellowship together for a long, long time.

I had to keep dabbing at tears between mouthfuls. I wanted to be grateful and cheerful, but the thought of what was about to be my fate held me prisoner as much as any jail could have. Bridget sat with me. Patience and Fear moved to another table to sit with Dorothy Bradford and other young women. Bridget and I wept openly, realizing this would be our last supper together for years to come. I am glad I did not know it was the last meal we should ever share.

I could barely swallow for the lump that settled in my throat. Yet, I wanted to treasure this offering of food. I also wondered how long it might be before I would taste such fine fare again. Bridget told me, "I shall put a bowl out for you when I make preparations for our meal. I will pretend that you have gone only for a moment to fetch something, and will be back shortly to converse with me, as we have so often done."

At that I put down my knife and made no further effort to stop the tears. Instead, I hugged Bridget and clung to her until Pastor Robinson's voice interrupted us. "Come, come, beloved. Though we shall soon part for now, we are one great fellowship with all the saints before, and the saints all around us even now. Put away your sorrow and rejoice in this day the Lord has given us." He began singing a familiar psalm and soon others joined him. It took me a bit, but I too joined, grateful to have the distraction.

"That was the sweetest melody that ever mine ears heard," Mr. Winslow said when the singing concluded and we prepared to move to the canal to embark on this grand adventure.

It took us only a few minutes. Others had already delivered our trunk. Everyone from the fellowship came to see us off all the way to Delft Haven where we boarded the *Speedwell*. Everyone had sacrificed what they could to purchase this old ship for our voyage and they were eager to inspect it. Some went aboard and nodded their approval of our community ship. Others were content to admire the ship from the dock.

My children and I spoke barely a word on the short boat ride to Delft Harbor. No words were adequate to convey the cacophony of emotions swirling within me. I felt like I was in a dream and if I could wake up, all this would disappear. This was not a dream at all, but rather, my fate. In a few minutes I would have to see the precious faces of Jonathan, Patience and Fear for the last time for a very long time, without William beside me to offer encouragement. Even Wrestling and Love seemed to sense the seriousness of this moment and were mercifully quiet and compliant. What I couldn't bear to tell the boys

Kathryn Brewster Haueisen

was the possibility of a disaster of some kind on the ocean; that we may never see them on this earth again.

I was amazed when we arrived at Delft Haven to see among the crowd a few friends and neighbors from our Amsterdam days. Some of the Leyden women carried baskets of food and handed them to us as we moved slowly toward the *Speedwell*. Pastor Robinson gathered us all together one more time for a farewell prayer. Dropping to his knees, he implored the Lord to watch over us until we should meet again, if not in this life, then in the eternal life where no more tears will be shed. He pleaded for a safe passage. I opened my eyes and looked around. Everyone was weeping. Again, I wondered how doing the will of the Lord could result in so much sorrow. I tucked that away, along with other feelings I dare not speak out loud, into my secret treasure chest.

I put Love and Wrestling in front of me and nudged them forward. Mr. Bradford assisted us. Dorothy was a pitiful sight and I wanted to offer her a bit of comfort. I wondered how it must hurt her to see me with my young boys when her own sweet little boy was back in Amsterdam with her parents. I resolved to show extra tenderness toward her once we were on our way. I stood on the deck of the *Speedwell* with Love and Wrestling on either side of me and my eyes fixed where only a moment ago I was embracing my other children.

All in all, some sixteen men, ten other women, and nineteen children pressed against the deck railing watching Holland slip away as we headed toward the open waters that would carry us back to England. I kept my eyes locked on where I last saw my children until the land was a blur and salt spray made my eyes sting.

Chapter 10

July 22, 1620

I shall write little now for the space is cramped and the ship rolls too much. I want only to write that we are on our way. That is, I, Love and Wrestling are on our way. I presume Jonathan, Patience and Fear are now back at the Robinson's. I trust William has made it to Southampton and is waiting to board the **Mayflower.** *In spite of the sadness at parting from my loved ones in Leyden, I feel a seed of excitement taking root. Soon I shall see William and we shall not be separated again in this lifetime. I hope.*

This was only my second time on a ship like the *Speedwell*. The first time I sailed with William and the three older children leaving the only home I had known up to that time in my life. Now, there was a hollow place in my heart where they belonged. My longing to see their faces, hear their voices, smell their presence pressed down on me until I had to fight to breathe.

On this voyage I traveled with my two young sons who had never been on a ship before. They were torn between their boyish curiosity about all aspects of this floating house, and their confusion and apprehension about leaving without their father, sisters or brother. They kept asking me when they would see their father again and I kept struggling to explain how a king was looking for him while trying to keep anger out of my voice.

I was grateful for my sons. They helped distract my racing thoughts. I tried to focus on the feel of the ship rolling gently and the wind in my face, but unwelcome images whirled around in my mind. What if we can't find William when we arrive? What if we sink? What if we are betrayed and turned into the authorities again? What if one of the boys falls overboard?

My thoughts changed direction when I heard a commotion among the crew. Though I knew little about ships, I recognized agitation well enough when I heard it. Sailors scurried this way and that, yelling words I didn't understand.

Mr. Bradford saw the look on my face and walked over to explain it. "I overheard Ship Master Blossom. The ship is leaking. Not too badly yet. We'll make it to Southampton, but no farther."

Leaking! My worst fears were now confirmed. I clutched my sons. Dorothy burst into tears. Wrestling yanked on my skirt. "Mama, are we going to die?"

Love tried to show his superiority and some humor by answering before I could, "No, fool. We're going to England!"

"Down below. Get down below!" The order came from a sailor who reeked of rum and tobacco. We made our way below deck and pressed against the walls of the ship, trying to make ourselves unseen. Sailors ran this way and that, doing tasks with a speed that alarmed me; their panic was easy to see as they hurried from one rope to a sail to something on a side port, I had no idea what they were doing, but there was not a set of hands or feet not in motion.

"We place our trust in God. God will deliver us," said Deacon Fuller. "We paid good money for this ship. I'm sure it will turn out well. We just need to stay out of the way and let the crew tend to her."

Kathryn Brewster Haueisen

"It won't be long until we see the shore of England," Mr. Bradford assured us.

Perhaps we did not have a mutual understanding of what we each consider *long*. We boarded the *Speedwell* on July 21 with the sun directly overhead. We didn't hear the first shouts of "land ho" for two days. I remember it was when shadows grew long and the sun was only a few inches above the horizon.

Ship Master Blossom approached. "You shall spend the night on the ship while me an' me men assess the damage. I shall inform you in the morning how long we shall be detained."

My heart sank low. I could see the *Mayflower* bobbing gently up and down. Was William on it? I stared at it until starlight replaced sunlight, hoping I might see him across the harbor. Resigned to another night where I was, I settled the boys for the night.

"When there is nothing we can do, the best course of action to do is nothing." Katherine Carver offered us her philosophy as we all settled ourselves down to wait.

~ ~ ~

The next morning, I looked around and realized that about half our fellowship had gone up to the deck. Hoping the boys would sleep a while longer, I quietly went up to see what this new day might look like from the open deck. The sun was barely above the horizon, but from what I could see, it was going to be a beautiful day. Streaks of pink, orange and light purple lit up the horizon.

The Bradfords stood around me. Mr. Bradford sighed. "We have left pleasant Leyden. Soon we are pilgrims and must lift our eyes to the heavens, our truest country." I was surprised how much the words of such a young man gave me encouragement.

At last, we were allowed off the ship while the crew addressed the leaks. I gathered up my sleepy sons and hurried onto dry land. We soon met the strangers foisted upon us by the investors, who seemed as uncertain about traveling with us as we were to travel with them. We introduced ourselves and exchanged what pleasantries we could muster.

Their Mr. Christopher Martin pushed his way to the front of the gathering. With an abrasive, bellowing voice, he shouted, "Attention! Lend me your attention. The Adventurers have appointed me to help with the final preparations. All you men gather here and await my instructions. You women may walk about a bit to savor doing so on land as we make ready to depart."

Mr. Winslow approached me and whispered, "I spoke with Mr. Carver. He reported efforts to work with these people go as well as you might anticipate a cat and dog cooperating. But, Mary, he will take you to see William. Come with me."

So, he made it to Southampton from London! Praise the Lord for that! My spirits lifted. New hope and energy coursed through me so strong I felt like I could float. I clasped each son with one of my hands and followed him through the crowd. We found William sitting serenely in a small room in a nearby house, with an open book on his lap.

I had to wait for Love and Wrestling to step back from assaulting him in their happiness and eagerness to see him again. When it was my turn, we embraced. It was sheer joy to feel his beard rub my cheek and feel his chest pressed against mine. My throat tightened with relief. I was speechless. All the afflictions of the past months melted away and I felt myself overcome with emotion. For months I fell asleep each night longing to be this close to my husband. Now that he was here before me, I hardly knew what to do. He patted the space next to him on the bed, inviting me to join him. Then he inquired about our journey as though this were all merely another, ordinary sort of a day.

It was a strange situation. I carried within me such frustration and animosity about the things I had been obligated to endure for so long, but my love for my husband lifted that like a breeze does to some morning fog.

We discussed what we should do next. It was obvious all of us could not spend the night in this tiny room. It barely contained him.

Kathryn Brewster Haueisen

Also, it was dangerous for him to be seen in public and if people knew we were here, someone may come innocently or otherwise to observe my situation. Searchers lurked everywhere. They would get a handsome reward for turning him in. So, we visited him each day, but stayed on the *Speedwell* at night while the crew made repairs. We made a big show of walking up and down the dock each night before boarding so that no one would notice we started near a particular small house. After a week, Mr. Carver arranged for me to move our things over to the *Mayflower,* anticipating we would sail in a day or two. We waited another week.

During this time of waiting, our investors, who we just called the Adventurers now, introduced us to the last minute extra people, including the More children. No one seemed certain of their situation. Some said they were orphaned. Others said their mother's husband was not their father and he wanted nothing to do with them. I evaluated the two assigned to me: Richard and Ellen. Servants, indeed. More like abandoned children in need of people to feed and clothe them. Now I had four children who required my constant supervision on a ship. As much as I resented the responsibility, I took pity on them. They looked terrified to me; perhaps expecting from me what they had already gotten from the many other adults who shuffled them around like sacks of rice. Apparently, their mother's indiscretions thrust them into the cruel circumstances of being unwelcome, unwanted and foisted on the sparse charity of people busy with their own lives.

Well, I knew how to manage children. After a few awkward minutes, it actually felt good to be tasked with doing something familiar in the midst of our peculiar circumstances. I showed them our area, introduced my sons and started to explain what the days would probably be like on the ocean and that it would be worth it once we landed and created our very own city. Their eyes were wide as they imaged creating something so grand.

One day while we were stranded on the docks, I asked Dorothy Bradford to watch all four of my charges so I could visit William alone to discuss something. I was getting worried about how long it was taking us to get underway. After months of sneaking to see him and knowing I was being watched, I felt some men were around the dock in hopes of catching my husband. How would he make the short but open distance from his hiding house to our ship?

He explained how he planned to slip onto the *Mayflower* in the midst of a large group of the Strangers and crew loading the ship with supplies. In the weeks to months while we waited, we began to refer to our sailing companions forced upon as Strangers as a way to distinguish them from our fellowship, the ships' crew and our investors. Because we used the word with calm respect, it seemed to stick to them and they took it on, just like we did with the name of Separatists.

William's plan was this: by hoisting bags of supplies over his shoulder, and with his head bent down, he could pass as just another passenger preparing for a long voyage. Once on board, he would find a place to hide and stay hidden until the ship was far enough out to sea that England was out of sight. Hopefully only our group of Separatists would be under close watch, and as a Stranger, he could get lost in the crowd.

"I shall let Mr. Carver know where I hide, and only him. This will be over soon, Mary. I feel it. We have dodged the devil and his plans to thwart us this long. Be strong, my dear. Be strong. I think it best now if we remain apart until we are safely away from England for good. You are correct, all of our fellowship is being watched."

More hiding. Well, I have plenty of experience with this. I left him to his books and slowly made my way to the *Mayflower*. My feet felt as heavy as lumps of coal as I reluctantly boarded the ship to wait.

Again.

Still.

More.

I was so very weary of it all. Yet the look in William's eyes when he called me his dear; it thrilled my heart and I was started to think ahead; what a joy to create a place to live where we could talk freely, act as we knew we were called to. I started to feel the adventure setting in.

Kathryn Brewster Haueisen

Chapter 11

August 5, 1620

> *This morning we finally began the voyage. After so many delays and so much waiting, I am relieved to be on the way. William is here on the ship somewhere. I know that from the very slow nod and smile given to me by Mr. Carver. The children are busy exploring the limited area where they are allowed to roam. When I go up on deck, I can see the **Speedwell** trailing behind us. At last, we are on our way.*

True to his word, Mr. Carver informed me that William was safely aboard. This was not as easy a task as I had thought it would be because Mr. Carver was always in the midst of a crowd. When I began to pace the rails as the moring ropes were tossed to the dock, I heard him clear his throat. As I turned toward him ready to rush over and beg him to wait for William to get to the ship, he nodded and smiled, then turned back to the swarm of people around him. I knew William was then in some storage area waiting for England to slip away. I was to act forlorn to give the impression to any spy (or anyone using a spyglass on another ship) that I had been abandoned. That was not very difficult.

I took all four of the children under my charge to the side rails where we could watch the wind fill the sails and smell the salty air as we sailed away from the busy coastline. Knowing we were all on the ship and on our way, I felt hopeful again. I focused on the *Speedwell* trailing along behind us and tried to imagine what the next few weeks would be like. What happened next turned out to be nothing like I had speculated.

~ ~ ~

I asked Mr. Carver how much longer before William would come out of hiding. "When we are out of sight of both England and any large ships other than the *Speedwell.*"

That was not the answer I wanted; but it was the only one I received. We were one week out when I noted we seemed to change direction. By then I had grown used to the ship turning this way and that to keep the sails full. Yet this seemed different. The ship seemed to turn completely around. When I realized we must be sailing back toward England, I rushed to a crew member, but none would bother to talk directly to me. I had to find a man in our fellowship to get a clear answer.

"*Speedwell* still taking on water. She needs more repairs." Nine words summed up my ocean-size exasperation. We were going back, which meant William would remain hidden. My heart sank. It was all I could do to keep from falling into utter despair.

Strangers and Saints alike groaned at this news. I couldn't be sure, but I think I heard someone from the Strangers cussing out Master Jones and threatening to toss him overboard. It was going to be a very long voyage. As if we lacked sufficient discouragement, Mr. Carver reported that Mr. Cushman was afflicted with some illness. "He reports

Kathryn Brewster Haueisen

it is like a bundle of lead crushing his heart more and more day by day since we first arrived at Southampton. He further states that he has grave concerns about the seaworthiness of the *Speedwell*. It appears we were able to purchase the ship because no others would. I pray it can easily be repaired and we can be on our way!"

Before my watering eyes the English coastline was growing larger and larger. We pulled into the harbor at Dartmouth. Talk turned ugly as we waited on shore for the crew to make the repairs. William stayed out of sight on the *Mayflower,* but nearly everyone else walked about Dartmouth discussing our situation and rendering conflicting opinions about what we should do.

"Our provisions disappear at an alarming rate," noted Mr. Carver.

"And that rascal Martin refuses to give an account of how he has spent our money," fumed Mr. Bradford. "He struts around like a dictator. He wanted to forbid any of us going ashore, perhaps afraid we would leave."

Our fellowship determined William must assume charge of all affairs related to the church since the Adventurer investors had not secured a pastor for us. Mr. Carver would serve as our governor; Mr. Martin as governor of the others, the Strangers. "We shall pray the Lord grants us fortitude to tolerate him," said Governor Carver.

The few times I heard him speak, I found this Martin man despicable in many ways, but I had too much to do each day with the children to pay him much mind. Since our fellowship men were also not happy with him, I left it to them to ensure he kept to only his assigned duties and left us be.

Each evening we received a report on the repair progress and prayed the mending would go faster.

At last, after nearly three weeks stranded in port for repairs, on August 23, 1620, the *Speedwell* was deemed seaworthy and we set out again for the New World.

~ ~ ~

We were once again surrounded by ocean in every direction. I kept looking at the ladder that descended deep into the bowels of the ship, hoping at any moment I might see the graying head of my husband approaching, having determined us far enough from the docks to come back out into the open. That is what I was doing when the word spread through the tween deck like an approaching thunderstorm. "Master Blossom reports the *Speedwell* leaks again. He makes haste to the nearest port. We must follow."

There were simply no words to describe my despondency. How could any of the men possibly consider this to be the will of God!?

We sailed to port in Plymouth. "It cannot be that this happened without some devious work of those devils who do all they can to discourage and detain us," Governor Carver growled.

Whether it be the devil's doing or horribly poor luck, Master Blossom declared the *Speedwell* unfit for the long voyage. We were faced with the option to abandon this foolishness or continue all together on one ship. Though I voiced my preference to no one, not even the Lord, I hoped we might all agree to abandon this plan. I preferred we sail back to the Lowland and admit failure rather than face the ocean and then a life in the wilderness. But I knew in my heart the men would want to keep going.

To continue west, we would do so all together in one ship. Everyone on the *Speedwell* bustled like bees to move their possessions to the *Mayflower*. I contemplated what would happen if I abandoned the ship here in Plymouth. Perhaps I could find a way to return to Nottinghamshire. Would the remnant of my family here in England accept me? Could I do it with four children? What if I took only my sons? If I showed up after all these years away with two children no one knew, would we be accepted? Or would rumors fly about my being unfaithful and running from shame? Rumors like that always flew faster than the wind. What if I left all the children behind and ventured off on

Kathryn Brewster Haueisen

my own? Would I be reduced to begging for food? Could I make my way alone in the world? Would William come looking for me? What story could I spin to explain myself? I had heard of women who dared to travel alone. Their stories never had a good outcome.

In typical William fashion, even in hiding, my husband sent a message to me. "Be strong, dear wife. All shall be well. All shall be well." He knew where my heart was, and somehow, I was always on his mind even in the midst of larger plans.

~ ~ ~

Mr. Cushman admitted defeat and reluctantly abandoned his plans to sail. I imagine his wife and child appreciated his decision and with his growing health issues he may not have survived the voyage. After all those numerous trips between Leyden and London to negotiate arrangements, coupled with the tedious task of procuring our provisions and coaxing what cooperation he could from Mr. Martin, Mr. Cushman gave up his hope of going to the New World.

I envied his ability to make his own decisions.

At last, on September 6, with all one-hundred and one of us crammed into the tween deck, plus William hiding somewhere below, we raised anchor and sailed away from the Plymouth port; our third, and by the mercy of the Lord, final departure from England.

We would not see land again for two months.

Chapter 12

September 7, 1620

Misery on the ocean. We are sailing now. The ***Speedwell*** *abandoned and everyone and everything on it crammed into this one ship. We have an area about the size of a good garden for all of us, plus all the animals that were supposed to come over on the* ***Speedwell.*** *Two dogs that bark whenever they are startled, which they often are because dogs are land creatures, not used to sailing. Chickens squawk from their cages. Pigs grunt and groan. Two goats try to out complain the others. How far we've fallen from the luxurious days at Scrooby Manor.*

Wrestling and Love wandered away from me so I was searching for them, thoroughly exasperated. How could I possibly lose track of two boys in such a small space? It was early in our voyage, only two sunsets since we left Plymouth. I still had not quite mastered the skill of walking on a rolling ship. I frequently latched onto someone or something, sustaining a few unsightly bruises along the way.

Katherine Carver clutched her stomach with one hand and with the other, pulled herself up the ladder ahead of me. She leaned over the rail, gagging and retching, making it just in time to avoid us having to clean up another mess. The sight and sound of it made my own stomach queasy, but I managed to keep everything down to continue in my search for my missing sons.

I saw them with William who was hugging and chiding them at the same time. I wanted to run to him, but between the pitching of the ship and the nausea, I had to make do with calling out to him. With an arm around each boy's shoulder, my three men came to me. William caught me when I tripped and nearly fell. "We are on our way, Mary! We are on our way. Come, let us find a corner out of the way of the crew where we can talk."

He spoke as one observing that it might rain; not as one who had been largely beyond reach for nigh onto a year. My relief at seeing him mingled with my agitation that he could be so casual about our circumstances. I nodded agreement and accepted his help descending a ladder. The boys descended with ease, as if they'd been living on a ship all their lives. I suppose they carefully observed the sailors and quickly imitated their movements. William descended next. "This way I shall catch you if you trip."

It was a civil gesture, but it grated me nonetheless. How did he think I had been coping for weeks on board without his help? A thought flashed through my mind. Perhaps the sailors were right to resent having women and children aboard. I would certainly never master moving about a pitching ship as they did, climbing up and down the tall masts all day and night.

Once we settled in the tween deck, I relaxed a little, with vexation displacing former concerns. "Well, finally, we are on our way and now you decide to discuss things with me, after all the decisions have been made." I spoke more sharply than I intended.

Before responding he turned to the boys. "Lads, I rejoice to be with you again and we shall have many hours to converse. For now, I wish to speak to your mother alone. I see Mr. Bradford is showing something to the other young passengers over there. I bid you go join them and report to me later what you find."

Kathryn Brewster Haueisen

Love and Wrestling slowly moved toward where the others were engrossed in some game.

William turned his attention back to me, but overlooked my tone. "I found our two lads exploring and chastised them properly. I told them that we shall be on this ship for many days and therefore, they must be proper gentlemen and stay out of the way of the crew. They assured me they shall do so."

It both amazed and annoyed me how quickly they comply with whatever William asked of them when I could never solicit such cooperation without raising my voice, and often threatening to report their disobedience to William.

William has always had the most disconcerting way of dispelling my bad temper. With no preamble or apology, he said, "Mary, I accept this is not how you imagined our lives would unfold. We make our plans, but our Lord reserves the right to change them. Think of Abraham when God called him to leave all that was familiar and venture out to places unknown. You have been my Sarah, faithfully coming with me to where I perceive the Lord leads us."

Of course, Sarah followed. She had even fewer choices than I had.

"And think about Paul and the other disciples. How many of them had to leave all that was safe and familiar to go out into places where they met with hostility, suspicion and even violence? Or Jonah and how the Lord sent him into that wretched city of Nineveh."

I started sobbing and could not stop. All the tensions, fears, resentments and challenges of the past year pushed to the surface and spilled out my eyes and nose. I wanted to point out that they didn't take young children with them or spend weeks in the middle of an ocean, well except perhaps Jonah. Jonah's story was hardly one I wished to experience for myself. I decided to withhold my thoughts. I said none of that. Rather I just cried. I think my breakdown tore at William.

He pulled me into his arms and stroked my hair, saying nothing for what seemed a very long time. Then he gently pushed me away so he could look into my swollen eyes. He wiped the tears off my cheeks and tilted my head up so our eyes met. "Oh, my dear, dear Mary. My Ebenezer. What trouble I have caused you. We have not undertaken this lightly. We prayed diligently to know the will of the Lord and for the strength to do what the Lord wills. We are convinced this is the path we are to pursue. So many others look to me for guidance and reassurance. In turn, I look to you for encouragement and solace. I trust I may always find what I seek in you."

I wept some more, but now the tears released my appreciation for the trust he placed in me. He did it again. He could always tame my sorrow, angst and anger.

He was right. I realized he relied on my support and compliance as much as I relied on his protection.

I felt tension slipping away, replaced with familiar feelings of security and serenity. I wiped my face dry with my apron and fell back into his arms. We didn't speak for several minutes, but somehow in that tender moment of embrace all the cares of the past many months evaporated and I remembered how much I loved him and how grateful I was to be his wife. Appreciation for the burdens he carried displaced my earlier aggravation. After all, I had only four young children looking to me to tend to their needs. He had our entire fellowship looking to him for guidance and relying on him to lead them to their future and the future that would nurture their grandchildren. For the first time since he left home to escape those searching to arrest him, I began to feel settled, as settled as I could manage on a ship in constant motion.

~ ~ ~

Our next challenge was monotony. Every day was like the day before and a preamble to the day to follow. Dreariness became a faceless enemy we fought with what few tools we had. We sang. The crew cursed us. We took turns gathering the children to teach them a few lessons. Noisy conversations all about interrupted us. William led us in

Kathryn Brewster Haueisen

prayer and worship. Crusty Master Jones called William into his cabin and forbid him to continue. Somehow William managed to use his persuasive skills to overcome the man's objections.

I reluctantly came to appreciate William's wisdom in leaving Patience and Fear safe in Leyden with the Robinsons. One day I caught one of the more repulsive sailors intentionally bump into poor Elizabeth Winslow and grope her. I reported the incident to William, but his only remedy was to suggest at least one of us older women accompany her whenever she ventured from the safety of our fellowship. I cringed to think Patience or Fear might have encountered similar situations.

The crew's crude behavior was soon overshadowed by another problem; we all began to stink and looked filthy. With water all around, we never realized this could be a problem, but the first time we pulled up buckets of seawater and then hung our clothes to dry, laughing at the dark grey water we tossed back into the sea . . . well we soon saw our problem. Our clothes dried hard, scratchy and stiff with salt. To wear off the salt was going to wear out the cloth too fast.

~ ~ ~

When we had been at sea two or three weeks—how hard it was to track the time—we decided to do wash again. We procured the use of two buckets and filled them both about two-thirds full of water from the communal water barrel. We used our own buckets to haul up sea water and did the main wash with this salty mix again, still laughing in triumph when we sloshed the dirty water back overboard. The first stage was done.

Taking turns, we dipped our things in the first bucket and sloshed them up and down. We had no access to a decent scrub board, so the water in the first bucket turned a grimy dark grey sooner than we hoped. We then dipped the items in the second bucket. We sent two of the older boys up to the top deck to dump the foul water overboard, with instructions to then refill the bucket with fresh water from the water barrel. The rinse buckets would need refreshing much faster than we supposed.

That was our plan, but the cook thwarted it when he found the boys at the water barrel. He swore at them, then bellowed at John Clarke. "Tell them bloody women to leave mi water barrel alone. We ain't hardly got 'nuff water as 'tis to last the whole bloody trip without them's wasting it on their dainties. I'll lash the next soul what touches our fresh water to the main mast and cut pieces off 'em to feed the crabs!"

The master's mate delivered the message. No more laundry until we reached land.

We were obliged to endure another smelly deprivation.

Kathryn Brewster Haueisen

Chapter 13

September 25, 1620

After many weeks at sea, I am accustomed to watching the skies for signs of how things are progressing on our voyage. Days that are too calm are as troubling as days when the skies are angry. Calm days mean little forward progress. But excessively windy days make the water treacherous. I observe the crew since they are adept at interpreting every cloud and adjusting the sails accordingly. I sensed from them one day that we were heading into trouble. They moved faster than usual and all their joking and poking fun at us came to a halt. They roused those sleeping in their hammocks and put them to work. I knew something was wrong before the waves even started growing higher and higher. The ship lurched front to back and side to side and the rain made everything miserable and slippery. I truly thought we would die that night. I prayed that if we did, we would all die together, and not be blown away from one another in the howling wind that shook the ship for hours.

Fear: "Fear! Fear! Tell it to us again! How we almost died!" This is the clamor I heard from my little brothers so often about this part of our family's story. For this episode, I will tell it still in my Mother's words, but I will add bits and pieces I learned from the others on the *Mayflower* that night of the big storm. Mother still pales when she talks of it, and never goes into the details that the boys love. Truth to tell, since I crossed the ocean later and weathered a few smaller storms, this part of my parents' journey also thrills me and makes my heart start to beat faster. Please forgive me if this story is more raucous than the rest; I blame it on my brothers and their imagination gone wild . . .

The ship's rolling grew worse; the wind blew colder. Sailors climbed high above the deck pulling ropes, taking down sails and calling out orders to each other. Some of the waves splashed over the top deck. The howling wind made it impossible to hear anyone. We huddled in the tween deck, terrified and powerless to do anything to help ourselves. Sailors tossed ropes to us and told us to tie ourselves to whatever we could find.

That was all the help they offered.

Two little children rolled across the tween deck before their parents could grab them. Their parents rushed after them, stumbling back with them, then lashed them to timber frames. They cried so loud I heard them over the wind. I looked up the ladder and watched the masts above us wave back and forth in wide arcs. Realizing how serious this was, we also tied our children together and then all of them to a beam. The waves crashing against the ship sounded like thunder and shook us to our bones.

Icy salt water poured over the railing and down into our area, soaking everything. Two sailors came down and stretched a long rope around poles and ladders for us to grab in case we needed to move about. We rode out the storm that way for what seemed forever.

Then sailors tossed buckets down the ladder and told the men to start passing them along to each other, hanging on to the ropes with

Kathryn Brewster Haueisen

one hand. The pumps could not keep up with the water coming in from the waves! Men formed a bucket brigade, passing sloshing buckets along a line to the open cannon ports. William untied himself and joined the effort. The men closest to the portholes pitched water back into the sea, and then a smaller line passed the empty ones back. All the while, the pumps below ran at full capacity.

With great effort, the bucket brigade barely managed to return as much water to the sea as the storm washed aboard. I sat with my arms around four terrified children. Darkness set in and not being able to see caused all our fear to grow. All I knew to do was close my eyes tight and pray this night would soon end. Of all the things I imagined might happen to us, drowning at sea in a storm was not one of them. Though, looking back, it should have been. I should have been fearful for I knew ships went down at sea all the time.

Mr. Hopkins was shipwrecked in 1609 on his way to Jamestown. I marveled that he wanted to make the crossing again, especially with his new wife Elizabeth expecting their baby any week now.

We would not be so fortunate as to be shipwrecked.

We were hundreds of miles from land.

If the ship could not withstand the pounding of this night, we would all go down with the ship and drown.

I heard a loud crack over the roar of the wind and waves. It sounded like a mountain split in half by demons. Then a boom. I couldn't even fathom what it might be. After that, all I heard was the raging storm. Whatever had just happened, the storm took supremacy again.

I looked around wondering if we had been hit by lightning and might die by fire rather than drowning. There was no evidence of such, besides, the rain was so heavy, a fire did not have a chance against it. I went back to doing the best I could to rock the children while all the men kept bailing water.

Sometime after midnight the rain let up a little. We learned that the loud noise had been the sound of the beam supporting the center mast cracking. It was only a few meters away from where I sat huddled with the children. The stress from the relentless wind and waves forced the ship to twist. The huge ship had her bow heading left, her stern heading right all the while the entire core of our world was going up on waves and slamming down in the troughs of giant waves. An hour of this had caused the enormous beam to buckle.

Soon a dozen or so sailors approached to inspect the scene. Their lanterns waved wildly as the ship was still pitching something fearful. One of the sailors lost his balance and fell right into the Hopkins family, landing inches away from Elizabeth's swollen belly. He cursed up a storm about the stupidity of letting women on the sip. Especially a woman with child. Elizabeth was tied to a pole, so she was defenseless. Stephen intervened quickly by pulling the sailor up. He got no thanks for his efforts.

Then another sailor fell, knocking his head hard on the tween deck floor. More swearing. That sailor cut his leg on something as he fell and started screaming for someone to get a rag to stem the bleeding.

Curses abounded.

I heard them clearly over the storm. The crew ignored the sailors that got hurt and instead continued to survey the broken beam by the light of their lanterns. I heard them say it would be impossible to keep sailing west. "Gotta turn back as soon as this calms a bit."

"Right you be mate. No way this old thing will make it all the way to the New World and back to England."

Meanwhile, the Separatist men huddled as far away as they could get from the crew to assess our situation. They were soon joined by the Strangers.

"We must convince Master Jones to keep sailing," insisted Governor Carver."

The Strangers' governor, Christopher Martin agreed. "We paid damn good money for this voyage. I'll not tolerate them turning back."

The wind finally dwindled to a strong ocean breeze. William helped me undo the ropes and settle the children on their sleeping pallets. The pallets were wet, but they didn't seem to notice or care. All of them soon dozed off, thoroughly worn out from the events of the

Kathryn Brewster Haueisen

past hours. I also dozed off, woken off and on in the dark by low voices.

When I woke once more there was a slight gray in the sky indicating morning would be here soon. I could easily hear our men talking. I leaned toward the ladder to hear more.

"We cannot turn back now!" insisted Governor Carver. "We must convince Master Jones to keep sailing west."

A voice I didn't recognize said, "The captain says we were two seconds from death. That he would keep his boots on to hold water and drown before the sharks could eat him. He is very disturbed. I heard him tell the crew that we are turning toward England, and to pray that beam don't split clear in two. If it does, we're all doomed for sure."

Mr. Bradford added, "Let us pray this will not end our plans."

Mr. Hopkins responded, "Of course this has ended our plans. Master Jones won't risk making the round trip with a cracked beam. Face reality!"

"We must help the crew," said Carver. "Though they distain us greatly, they are in sore need of our Lord's help. That help will come through us and the preparation we did under God's eye for our new colony. We must pray that the Lord will come to their aid, and thereby it will also be to our aid."

At just that moment Master Jones walked nearby. Mr. Carver rushed over, clutching the captain's arm to slow him. "We have with us a giant iron screw. We brought it to build what structures we might require. We thought perhaps your cooper, young mister John Alden, might use it."

"We are all doomed if we can't repair the beam. Not sure we can even make it back to England. But England is closer and our best chance now. No way we can make it to the New World and back. Now you tell me this?! What are the chances a giant tool found only in shipyards is on my ship? If it's what I think it is, we might finally have a stroke of luck."

Shaking his head, the captain then growled, "I will have Mr. Alden begin the repair at the crack of dawn, he has only one day to prove the repair will hold or we return you all to England. Mr. Alden must attest that the repair will hold not only to the New World but back again to England. Otherwise, I will lock any of you up who try to stand in my way. I don't plan to die trying to get you to your colony."

~ ~ ~

We knew it wasn't luck, but the intervention of our faithful Lord that provided for the repairs and allowed us to sail on to the New World. After that night we returned to the monotony of slowly making our way across the sea, one dreary day after another. After the excitement of that night, boredom was a most welcome travel companion.

~ ~ ~

There were other storms to mitigate the boredom; but none as violent as the night the main beam cracked. But one other storm did make me wonder if I should ever see land again. One of our members, the man servant to our beloved Governor John Carver, didn't come below quick enough when a storm started pitching our ship about like a toy. Poor John Howland got tossed overboard. He would have drowned for certain if the crew hadn't spotted him straight away. The crew never tried to mask how much they resented us; but they weren't about to let a man overboard sink to the bottom of the sea without a fight. The ship was at such an angle to the water that Howland managed to latch on to the topsail halyards. He clung to it for dear life long enough for the crew to haul him back on board with a boat-hook.

Then back to the tedium of the same monotonous routine day after day. In October, when we had been at sea for six weeks, we had a most welcome distraction from the tedium of the restless ocean.

Kathryn Brewster Haueisen

Chapter 14

October 7, 1620

I think of how I labored when each of my children were born and marvel at the force of life. Regardless of our horrid conditions, when the good Lord is ready to bring forth new life, neither man nor nature shall prevent life. Poor Elizabeth! She certainly has a story to tell that matches that of her husband's shipwreck adventures.

We were already a full month behind our planned arrival and all hopes of reaching land before our three pregnant mothers should deliver were long since dashed. William and other foolish men had attempted to reassure the expectant women we would see land before their time, but I surmised it was a false hope, spoken in a vain effort to lighten their fears. Perhaps they believed what they spoke. I didn't, yet would not contradict so directly my husband. As September turned toward October, Elizabeth Hopkins spent hours each day walking about the crowded tween deck area, holding her hands beneath her expanding midriff. She often lost her balance and had to grab a hold of whoever was closest or risk falling.

On a cold, overcast early November morning, she began to moan and rub her back. We were in the middle of the ocean, and she was going into labor! Several experienced mothers tended to her, but we had scant to offer in the way of comfort. The Hopkins were one of the few families among us who could afford to have their own cabin, so Elizabeth's situation was as good as it could be on a rolling ship.

Priscilla Mullins approached the cook to request hot water, which he reluctantly provided, after scolding her for needing it. "Bloody women got no business being on a ship! Scandalous. Ain't never seen nothing like it. Never want to again! Take your bloody water and git out my way."

Priscilla was shaking from the cook's abruptness when she returned and reported his angry outburst. There was no way we could avoid this odious, grumpy man. This baby was on the way. Perhaps we could think of a way to make nice toward him later. Now all our attention was focused on bringing this new soul into the world and keeping it and the mother alive and as healthy as we could.

We added additional sleeping pallets around Elizabeth so she could prop herself up with a bit more comfort. Her birth pangs came more frequently, screams of pain we knew were so loud they passed through the door with ease. The callous sailors cursed at her every time she cried out, offended by the sounds of bringing new life into the world. They were too ignorant to realize this was how they began their own thankless lives.

Finally, she pushed her baby into the light of his own new world. He greeted us with a lusty cry, and we all clapped. I heard a cheer coming from the others who waited near, anxious to know if the baby would be born alive. Stephen stepped into the cabin where Elizabeth was now propped up holding their new son. Both parents were beaming with relief that her ordeal had ended happily. She clutched the baby to her breast, and asked, "What name shall we give him?"

"Oceanus," said Stephen with a certainty that indicated he'd been thinking of a suitable name as he paced and waited.

Kathryn Brewster Haueisen

William peeked into the cabin to ask if they would like him to offer a prayer of thanksgiving. "Though we are not of the same religious preferences, we are all surely equally thankful for this gift of life."

Stephen nodded smiling like a fool.

William prayed.

Master Jones wrote in the ship log:

Mistress Elizabeth Hopkins, wife of Master Stephen Hopkins of Billericay, in Essex, was delivered of a son; who, on account of the circumstances of his birth, was named Oceanus, the first birth aboard the ship during the voyage. A succession of fine days, with favoring winds.

~ ~ ~

After the Hopkins baby was born, time again dragged on.

Some among us never adjusted to life at sea. The poor Button lad was sick most of the voyage. His condition continued to worsen until he rarely left his pallet. Deacon Fuller, his master, was also our doctor. Nothing he tried gave the boy any relief.

Even Dr. Giles Heale, part of Master Jones' crew, couldn't find a remedy for the boy. From his frown and restless walking about I suspected Deacon Fuller questioned coming with this first group from our fellowship. He spoke frequently and fondly about his wife Bridget, back in Leyden. I wondered what my life would have been like if William would have allowed me to stay with the Robinsons instead of coming with him on this pilgrimage.

Thinking to let Deacon Fuller rest, and to occupy Dorothy Bradford's empty hands, I suggested she and I sit with his servant a spell. Traveling alone, he lacked a private cabin and made do with a designated place in the open area of the tween deck like most of us.

It was early November and a chilly, overcast day. I found a lantern, and we made our way to the shadowy corner where the Button boy lay. He seemed unaware of us or his surroundings. We sat quietly with him, stroking his forehead, and humming little bits of hymns I thought might comfort him. He slipped away that day, as we sat on either side of him. I was on my way to tell Deacon Fuller when Dorothy called after me, "Do you hear that? What are they saying?"

Loud voices from the upper deck drifted down to us. I moved closer to the ladder to hear better. "Look! Look! Look what I found!" Francis Billington had hold of a small bird by its tiny legs and was swinging it round and round. It was dead, no doubt from the exertion of flying all the way out to sea, but it was our first sign that we might finally come to land again.

William approached the Billington youth to inspect the bird for himself. Then he announced, "We must gather everyone to pray. This is surely a sign of land. May I have the bird?"

Francis reluctantly handed the dead bird to William, who I presume wanted to show it to Mr. Bradford and some of the others. Perhaps this type of bird could tell the sailors or Master Jones something about how close we might be to land.

I found Deacon Fuller and told him the news about his servant and the dead bird on the deck. He sighed deeply. "Two deaths in one day. One marks a boy's life too soon gone; another brings the assurance we near the end of our crossing. The Lord giveth and the Lord taketh. Blessed be the name of the Lord." He walked away, shaking his head as he went. I strained my eyes to the west but saw only what I always saw; the endless sea and sky.

~ ~ ~

Kathryn Brewster Haueisen

Three days later I stood on the top deck watching the sailors adjust the sails. I stayed until I could not bear the cold a moment longer. I rounded up the More children and our sons and insisted they come back to the tween deck with me. The children begged to stay on the main deck, but I feared William would not keep an eye on them if he engaged in conversation with the other men. Wrestling started to sass me, but William appeared just then and put his hand on Wrestling's shoulder. Without saying a word, he turned him toward the entrance to the tween deck. Wrestling reluctantly descended.

Though we traveled as a family, we did not have the luxury of a cabin. We made a spot for ourselves with some of our things making partial walls to separate us from the others who traveled in the same lowly conditions as ours. Settled into our little space now, I listened to the crew. Those high up in the maze of ropes and sails called down to those on the deck working the ropes. They in turn called out to Master's Mate Robert Coppin, who advised Master Jones. Master Jones sent instructions back through the same chain. I was content to listen to them from what little warmth the tween deck afforded me. At least in the tween deck I was away from the biting mist and wind.

Then I heard a sailor from high up on the mast call out two of the most glorious words I ever heart. "Land Ho! Land on the horizon! Land Ho!"

"Land!" A spontaneous cry of delight erupted everywhere, all over the ship. A chorus of cheers and laughter sounded out as we repeated *land* again and again. It was as sweet a sound as I ever heard. The younger folks even grabbed one another with hooked elbows and began dancing! It was a sight I shall never forget. I had not sufficiently appreciated what a blessing it is to have solid ground beneath me. I was oddly surprised that the sailors seemed as thrilled to sight land as we landlubbers were. I suppose the near sinking of the ship from the broken beam in that massive storm had them all wanting a respite from the ocean.

Many of us were already on the upper deck preparing for what bit of dignity we could offer the Button boy. His corpse was already wrapped in a sheet and at rest on the board, balanced on the edge of the rail. Master Jones insisted it was his place to say something over the body before releasing it to the sea.

In all the commotion and excitement someone, whether on purpose or not, pushed the recently departed Button lad over the rail to his final resting place. When I heard about it, I was stunned. Such a sad life for the little boy, to die so far away from family and so close to our destination. He should have had a proper burial. But what was done was done. William quietly offered a prayer of commendation for the dead once Master Jones turned to tend to other matters. He did not want to incur any more of the crusty man's wrath.

We continued slowly sailing toward the coast.

I strained to see land for myself, but all I saw was darkness gradually pushing the last of the daylight over the horizon, out of sight. Waves slapped against the ship and the sound made my eyelids grow heavy. By the time the first stars peeked through the clouds my longing for sleep overcame my eagerness to see land.

That night we all went to sleep dreaming of waking up to the sight of a coastline.

~ ~ ~

The next day our men met with Master Jones in his cabin. William returned looking grave and defeated. "We are many miles from the Hudson River. He insists for now our best chance is to return to a bay he heard about that is not far."

I did not know how to respond, so I said nothing.

It felt serious, yet we arrived, and land was in sight. Surely the hardest part of the journey was over. He explained further after seeing I had no concept of the issue.

"The seas here are rough and Master Jones worries we cannot safely reach the river this late in the year. It would be most hazardous to

Kathryn Brewster Haueisen

sail toward the Hudson. We must sail north, away from these agitated waters. He says he was told about a protected cove just on the other side of the land we have been sailing past, a place where he can drop anchor away from the rough seas. We must pray it is still in the territory of the Virginia Company, or we may have to spend the entire winter on the ship and then sail again south along the coast. If this happens, the merchants could decide to charge much more for the voyage, and that could add years of servitude to our dept."

We made it across the Atlantic Ocean. Through a storm so evil it nearly stopped us, with one man overboard and mercifully pulled back from the sea. We'd helped Elizabeth Hopkins safely deliver Oceanus. Somehow my normal tendency to worry was diminished. I just knew, knew to my core, that the Lord was going to deliver us to a spot where our fellowship would be able to build and grow and thrive in the light of his love.

Besides, anything had to be an improvement over this floating, endless confinement. Knowing the seas were getting rougher, I was pleased when Master Jones turned the ship north again, then west, then south, and finally east, where we at last we sailed into a little cove. I saw land on three sides. The shipmaster assured us he checked his instruments and we were within the correct territory and could settled in this area. Later I wondered if he knew the truth, but did not want to face an angry ship full of irate passengers.

I asked William if that meant we were at our final destination. He shrugged. "It appears so. We are in the New World! Let us give thanks for that! I believe Master Jones may come to feel regret for how this has turned out. He offered us use of his longboat to explore a bit. Perhaps we will find good water here. We are nearly out of beer and certainly cannot drink saltwater."

Always his first response to any situation, William summed us together for prayers.

He thanked the Lord for guiding us safely thus far and bid the Lord grant our leaders the wisdom of King Solomon to discern what our next course of action ought be. When he finished, most of us joined the Strangers at the railing peering across the bay. We strained to see details along the shore, speculating on what might lurk there in this strange new place.

The sun kissed the land, bidding it good night, and slipped past the horizon.

Kathryn Brewster Haueisen

Chapter 15

November 12, 1620

We had been so long without sight of land, it felt strange to again see the sight of some sort of shrubs lining a shoreline. I wanted nothing more than to be off the ship, but naturally, it fell to the men to explore first and ensure it was safe for women and children to disembark.

More waiting!

At least the ship is steadier and I can see land.

Master Jones dropped anchor November 11, 1620, near the end of the day. When the sun returned in the morning it cast a lovely glow over the cove that protected us from the rigors of the sea. Other than the lapping water against the hull of the ship, it was silent, as silent as a group of over a hundred can be. The quiet ended abruptly.

Angry voices erupted overhead. William went to investigate, soon returning to explain the cause. "It seems those who are not of our fellowship believe that, having arrived not at our intended destination, nor within the territory granted by our charter, they are now free to part from us and go their own ways. The Strangers claim any agreements made with the Virginia Company are null and void. This is particularly the opinion of those who agreed to work with us as indentured servants, indebted to the company for seven years. Others insist since they paid for passage to a place which is now apparently beyond our reach, they owe allegiance to no one other than themselves."

I was appalled. How would we survive if over half the people left?

As if reading my mind, William assured me, "We convinced those who think thus that we must stay together. Some have suggested Master Jones intentionally sailed us off course. I prefer not to judge the man without solid evidence; but regardless, we are beyond the boundaries of the Virginia Company. We are quite literally in unchartered territory. We know little about this land, what wild beasts or other dangers may lurk close by waiting to finish us off before we begin. One of the Strangers reminded us that we were at the very start of winter. He encouraged the others of his group to stay together. We implored, aye, insisted, that we should certainly all die if we do not work together.

"Even Mr. Martin agreed we needed some sort of covenant to define how we should now come together as one community. Though he continues to feel the need to object to how we worship, I am confident we will win him and the others over with kindness and charity. We will meet again tomorrow to work out the details of our covenant. Mr. Carver shall serve as governor over all of us, with such assistants as we must soon decide."

That is how we came to be governed by the tenets of a compact forged on the *Mayflower* when we first rested at sea in the harbor at Provincetown.

~ ~ ~

Kathryn Brewster Haueisen

Being constrained to concern myself more with matters of the stomach than governance of the colony, I left William and the other men to their task. I went to the food barrel, where I again confirmed that indeed our supplies were dangerously low. A bit of cheese, some dried fruit, salted fish and pork. I chose a few dried apples and some prunes. That would have to do.

As soon as Love saw me, he commenced pestering me to go to land, to set his feet upon soil and explore whatever astonishing plants and creatures he might find there. His pleas were so earnest, he and I climbed to the upper deck to survey the land. It wrapped around our ship like an arm extending a protective hug. Master Jones was calling out orders to the crew.

Love mimicked, "Check the anchor's secure now, lads. We come to the voyage end. Tie those sails down good 'n tight. No need for them for a spell. Hear me?" I had to laugh at how closely his words copied the crew.

Then Love begged again about going ashore.

I suspected nothing more would happen until the men finished their work, I would have to distract my son for probably a few days. I never thought we would arrive and still have to wait. Now, looking into the low trees casting leafless black shadows, I realize how danger could be in every hollow! The men certainly must go ashore first to explore and set us a camp first.

Back in the tween deck, I guided the children through their morning routines, happy it was one of the last mornings I would have to do so. I divided the scant portions of food, trying not to acknowledge the fingers of fear wrapping around me when they asked for more. Longing for more would not make it appear. We had to get along with considerably less than we wanted.

The long delay leaving England put our food supplies in a sorry state.

If we didn't find something to eat in this barren winterscape, we would soon have no provisions to divvy up. At least there would be deer to hunt until we could find plants and berries after winter. Even when spring arrived, it would still be many weeks before a garden would yield food.

A long, lean time lay before us.

Kathryn Brewster Haueisen

Chapter 16

November 13, 1620

Yesterday they finished the covenant. From this day forward we shall no longer be our groups of Separatists Saints traveling with the London Strangers. We are now the Plimoth Plantation.

I like the sound of that. After all these weeks I have become rather fond of the women among the Strangers. We share more common concerns and interests than differences. We all plan how to provide for our children and how we can possibly make homes for them out of this forested landscape stretching as far as the eye can see.

I recall how agitated we were when we learned our investors were insisting we include total strangers to travel with us. Little choice did we have. We would have to accept them or forfeit our plans. Now that we've lived together in the cramped quarters of the ship for these many weeks, we remain Saints from Leyden and Strangers from England, but we are transformed into a new group of settlers. William reminds me that the Lord's ways are often not our ways. "The Lord in his infinite wisdom knew we would need help and has provided it through these Strangers."

The men emerged from their negotiations shortly after midday on November 12. William smiled as he reported the outcome. "Every single man has signed it, Mary! We have a plan going forward. And Master Jones instructed his crew to put the longboat in the water and take a few of our men to shore. Shore!" He clasped my hands and twirled me around a few times. "We have arrived, Mary. Lord Almighty, we are arrived. The Lord has been faithful to us."

As soon as word spread about going ashore, the women piled our dirty laundry into sheets tied together to make sacks. We planned to take these to ashore.

When William saw this, he pointed out, "You ought not count on venturing ashore just yet. We do not know what dangers lurk there. We must let the expedition party explore first."

I dropped my bag and plopped down on it with my heart bruised and my arms crossed. Though I tried to hold them back, tears overflowed onto my cheeks. I snapped. Leaving two homes, living alone while my husband hid out, leaving my children in Leyden, taking care of the abandoned More children . . . and now to be denied a chance to go ashore and do a little laundry. It was too much. With my head on my knees, I sobbed. I learned later many other women did as well. Months later we would joke about it; but at the time it nearly broke us. Often people collapse near to the end of making their dreams come true.

When I looked up, I saw the crew lower the long boat, followed by sixteen young men climbing down a rope ladder into it. A few were from our fellowship, a few more from among the Strangers, and the rest crewmen. I felt utterly defeated sitting on my bag of laundry as I watched them head for solid land.

As I sat there I recalled one loss after another; adding each to a litany of sorrow like kindling to a fire, until flames of repressed fury erupted in an outburst that shocked me as much as William. I stood, wiped my cheeks with the back of my hands, and risked it all to give words to my profound disappointment. I ignored the likely consequences: finger-shaped red marks on my cheek; bruises beneath my frock; even the shame of being coerced to publicly confess my disobedience to my husband. He had never so treated me in the past but neither had I ever spoken so boldly before. I suppose the long confinement at sea led me to speak my mind fully. No fear of his reaction was sufficient to hold back the tidal wave of emotion.

"William. I and the children, and the other mothers, and their children. We would rather be swallowed by wolves or bears than spend one more minute on this smelly ship when we can see land. Right there!" I pointed. I clinched my fists. "We have endured months with nothing clean to wear. We are surrounded by our own stench. It is a sunny day. We would wash our clothes! Is that too much to grant? After all the deprivations . . . all the danger we faced . . . all to follow *you* . . . and the other men . . . on this grand adventure? You all dream of some glorious new community in the wilderness. All *I* want is something to wear that does not reek with disgusting offensive odors." I put my hands on my hips and waited, expecting at least a tongue lashing. Perhaps far worse.

William is seldom at a loss for words, but that day, he was, for a moment. He stared at me as if trying to fathom who I was. Indeed, I hardly recognized myself. I know not from whence came the courage to speak so bluntly to my husband.

The others stood silently, waiting, afraid to move or speak until they knew which way this should turn out. A silent crowd of women, each with laundry at her feet; all staring at William.

William swiveled his head, looking at all of them as if waking from a deep sleep. He looked at each woman one at a time, studying her face, seeing the strain we were all under.

At last, he cleared his throat, looked at me, and stroked his goatee, as if doing so might pull up a response that would calm rather than further agitate me. "I did not grasp the urgency of your plan." He turned to the other women. "Is this how all of you regard the situation?"

All nodded agreement without speaking.

"Then I shall talk with Captain Standish to see if tomorrow he will assign a few men to escort you to tend to your work." He turned abruptly and disappeared into the bowels of the ship.

I looked at the other women who were smiling. I felt lighter, and clean inside, even though I was still wearing filthy garments, like when a storm passes and the air smells sweet. A collective sigh came out, there would be no beating or shame brought on me and we now had a definite goal for the next day.

~ ~ ~

The men returned just before sunset, excited with tales about all they found.

As head of their military defense, Captain Standish gave the report. "Sandy ground, with good black topsoil not far back from the beach area, more 'n a spade deep. We saw dunes like the ones in Holland."

Mr. Hopkins added, "And trees: oaks, pines and juniper. We brought back the juniper for a fire on the ship."

William cleared his throat. "And did you any see anyone?"

Captain Standish shook his head. "Not another person or sign of habitation."

The cook added the juniper to what little firewood he had left, and it did seem to ease some the horrid stench in the tween deck.

I rested well that night, wondering what it would be like to walk on land tomorrow.

Kathryn Brewster Haueisen

Chapter 17

November 15, 1620

My hopes of soon being done with this ship were premature. I can see land, and yesterday we at long last had a chance to escape a few hours to take in fresh air and walk on solid ground. It will be many more weeks before we have any suitable shelter built. Some of the men are now reassembling the shallop while others go off to explore. Perhaps that will result in procuring more food.

It breaks my heart to tell the children they have received all the food they will for this day. If William realized this would be our fate, might he have reconsidered this pilgrimage?

Suzanna White and Mary Allerton, both ready to deliver at any hour, looked crestfallen as several of us prepared to go to shore for a laundry day. Sarah Eaton bounced one-year-old Samuel in one arm while balancing a sack of laundry in the other.

"Surely you don't intend to take little Samuel to shore!" I said in a way that I hoped convinced her of the folly of such a plan. She begrudgingly conceded keeping an eye on a crawling baby while doing laundry would not be easy.

"I could go if someone would watch baby Samuel?"

Suzanna sank down on a stool and wrapped her hands around her swollen stomach. "I suppose I could do that for you. Resolved must become accustomed to having a baby demanding more of my attention. Do you think Resolved might go with you to shore?" I agreed to watch over her five-year-old. What bother could one more little lad be atop the ones I already had to watch?

Sarah handed Samuel to Suzanna who then perched him atop her bulging belly. Mary reached out to take Oceanus from Elizabeth so she could join our outing away from the ship. It was agreed, Suzanna White and Mary Allerton would tend to the babies in exchange for the rest of us doing their laundry.

I felt like I was taking a sweet away from a little child when I gazed upon Suzanna's downcast eyes and turned down lips. I knew she and Mary longed to go with us to shore, but with their babies due any day, it was out of the question. They would first have had to ascend from the tween deck up the stairs to the main deck; then climb down a wobbly ladder into the longboat, and finally step over the side of the longboat onto the shore, most likely getting their feet and skirts wet at best and falling down at worst.

We hugged them and promised to share every detail when we returned. Though we started the voyage as strangers, our long days confined in such congested conditions changed our opinions of one another. We had talked and shared experiences all wives and mothers have in common. That forged good friendships and cooperation.

Rose Standish, Mary Martin, Elinor Billington, Alice Mullins and her daughter Priscilla from the Stranger's group joined me, Dorothy Bradford, Katherine Carver and Elizabeth Winslow, along with others I cannot recollect now from our Separatist group. We took our bags full of filthy things, along with the children, and climbed into Master Jones' longboat.

Kathryn Brewster Haueisen

A few of his crew and three of our men rowed us across the bay. I felt giddy as the men rowed. I savored the breeze on my face and the fishy-smelling aroma of the water. I put my hand into the water. It was frightfully cold, but it felt wonderful to feel the water moving along my hand. I felt a shiver of pleasure with each stroke of the paddles, bringing the land closer and closer. When we reached land, the men jumped into the shallow water and shoved the boat up onto the shore so we could disembark without getting wet.

Those first few hours away from the ship were among the happiest I had known since leaving Leyden. The earth seemed to sway beneath our feet. We laughed at each other staggering about like men leaving a tavern. We slowly stumbled our way inland for a while until we came upon the freshwater pond the exploration party had found. Three men, with their muskets, accompanied us, so I felt safe and truly free for the first time since the magistrates came searching for William.

The children were even more excited. I had to use my sternest mother voice to remind them, "You must stay where you can see us. If you do not see us, we cannot protect you. Do you understand? If you cannot see us, you must come back immediately. If you do not, you shall lose your privilege to leave the ship again."

Mercifully, they obeyed. Their excitement was contagious. They would run yet totter and stumble from months on the ship, some fell to the ground laughing because they couldn't walk straight. I felt like running myself, but feared I would fall too, so I settled for delighting in their youthful energy.

The gloriously chilly temperatures turned my hands red as I dipped them again and again into the pond, but I didn't mind. It was a reminder that I was kneeling on solid ground and would soon know the scent of freshly laundered garments.

We sang and hummed as we worked, watching the children run and run, exuberant to be free of the constraints of the ship. Though I was chilled through and through, it was a magnificent day. As the shadows grew long, the crew reversed their work and carried us back to the ship.

That evening I debated whether I ought speak of my outburst with William. He is not one to hold a grudge, and I suspected he may not even remember it what with everyone's jubilation about going to shore for the first time. Yet, I felt embarrassed at my angry tirade which was not becoming of the loyal wife I hoped to be.

He broached the matter before I could decide, apparently observing something different in my manner. "And now that you have been ashore, is all better with your soul, Mary?"

Was that a rebuke? Or a sincere inquiry about my wellbeing? Even after all our years together, I still sometimes struggle to interpret his meaning. I confirmed I was indeed feeling better.

Then, so typical of William, and why I remain grateful I said *I will* that long ago day in Scrooby, he said, "I overlooked how all this must be from your experience. I do not mean to do so, but you have shown me that I do. I could not bear the burden of my responsibilities as their Elder if I could not count on you to be my helpmate. Forgive me that I do not tell you that often enough. You have kept us all fed and as well clothed as possible, while keeping the children safe and encouraging the other women. Your work truly is the foundation for me to be able to perform my own duties."

So like him!

No wonder so many in our fellowship look upon him as their own brother or father or uncle. Just when I muster the courage to finally say what often swirls round and round in my mind, he blows my feelings of discontent away like a feather on the wind with a few tender words. I find it impossible to remain angry with him for long.

Kathryn Brewster Haueisen

Chapter 18

November 20, 1620

The situation is better now that we are anchored in the cove. This offers us a bit of protection from the biting November cold. The men seem energized with the tasks of exploring the area and repairing the shallop. I feel better knowing that while 'tis a challenging situation, clean garments are the first step toward a new life.

William began our first service anchored in the harbor with a long prayer of thanksgiving for our safe arrival. At the start of our voyage, the crew mocked us when we gathered to pray and sing. The Strangers among us, all loyal to the Established Church we sought to escape, either gathered elsewhere, or stayed behind us, making a show of yawning and fidgeting through our service. They preferred the stiffness of their formal ways; we preferred our simpler and surely cozier ways of worshipping. While they seemed to love the extravagant trappings of their clergy, we appreciated the simple garb and more down-to-earth approach of our pastors, who came close to us and talked to us a equals.

After the night of that horrific storm, Master Jones lessened his resentment toward us a bit. I never heard of any thank you from him, but he must have been grateful for the help we were able to render. He retained his gruff ways, but no longer protested when we wanted to sing psalms or hold prayer services. William said this was further proof the Lord worked good out of calamity.

The frigid November weather made it nearly impossible to focus on William's prayers. I tried sending him mental messages to shorten his observations about our situation, but he meandered on, and on, and on. He preached about the ancient Israelites crossing the Red Sea, Joshua bringing down the walls at Jericho and Jesus keeping the devil at bay for forty days in the desert.

We dutifully listened, as was our custom to always respect whoever spoke with an open Bible and heart full of passion. Yet, I suspect every one of us from old Mr. Chilton to the youngest children thought more about our own situation than that of our ancient forbearers. We were anxious to establish our settlement and send Master Jones and his crew back to England. However, being the Sabbath, we contented ourselves to gather for worship, rest and wonder what our lives might be like in the months to come.

At the afternoon prayers, Mr. Carver reminded us that we had several crucial tasks before us. Our shallop was useless until it was reassembled. While the carpenters worked on that, another search party was created to explore the area further. Our food and water supplies were nearly gone and Master Jones was not inclined to share with us any of what he had set aside for his crew. He needed it all and more for their return voyage.

Given the unique situation in which we found ourselves, William and Governor Carver agreed that organizing the men into teams on the Sabbath would not be a violation against the admonishment to refrain from work. Talking and planning would be acceptable. The men would have to build homes for us from whatever

Kathryn Brewster Haueisen

they found available. We brought tools for building, but no building materials. Mercifully, it appeared the land contained an abundance of trees. Talk went from how to have a main place to start us out while cottages were built to which men would be on whose hunting party.

The next day some of the men dragged the shallop pieces to shore, one at a time, in the longboat. Cooper John Alden predicted it would take him and his helpers at least two weeks to reassemble the shallop. Their evening reports became a regular part of our daily routines. Their valiant efforts didn't always go smoothly. Cooper Alden reminded us one evening, "The cold and rain hinder us, and we must wait for high tide to get from the ship to shore and back. Each day seems to put a new challenge in our way."

William sighed each time they set off again, suggesting he ought to go with them. Young Bradford kept assuring him he was needed more on the ship to console those suffering from the ravishes of food shortages and damp bedding. "Your words always offer comfort. We ought not risk you also succumbing to the sickness that has latched onto some."

He asked me what I thought. A rare opportunity to express my truest thoughts. I pondered how best to phrase it. Finally, in a flash of inspiration I can only attribute to the Lord hearing my pleas for help, I told him, "I know it offers me and the children great comfort having you near us. Many others tend to the physical needs of our fellowship. You alone have been set aside to tend to our spiritual ones. I urge you heed the council of Mr. Bradford."

Work progressed slowly on the shallop. William went to shore only occasionally to encourage and thank those who labored so on our behalf. He spent most of his time talking to those on the ship who needed his strength of spirit. I was greatly relieved that he accepted a less strenuous part for himself. Neither of us were young anymore.

~ ~ ~

All the while Master Jones focused on how soon he could pull anchor and set sail for England, telling us often, "Never should have agreed to bring you here. None of you be fit for the challenges. Me and my men have to start back. We have barely enough supplies to make it if we leave now. You better find your place and settle it." Then he would stomp off to his cabin and slam the door.

His crew often talked openly in front of us as if we were deaf and dumb and did not speak their same English tongue. One day I overheard Master's Mate Clarke confiding in Master's Mate Robert Coppin. "Wish I'd ne'er agreed to this voyage. Wouldn't if the pay weren't so good. Can't earn this kind of pounds in ten trips up and down the coast back home."

"Right you are. But I didn't count on all the problems—his nasty moods especially."

"I think he was misled by the investors. Made 'im a lot of promises their investors won't likely keep. And I'm with him worrying about the low larder level. Not much chance we'll get much in this forsaken place to restock."

Master's Mate Coppin turned to stare down into the salty water below where they stood. "Plenty of fish, but no more way to catch more 'en a few now and then."

Hearing them talk I almost felt a twinge of pity for Master Jones. He for certain wasn't used to dealing with run-about children and crying babies. Nor listening to prayer services and hymn singing. And, he had a barrel of his own problems to solve. But still, his rudeness and crudeness were in need of some serious reform. I hoped that in time William might be successful in soothing a few of his ruffled feathers.

As for me, I much preferred being at anchor in the harbor over sailing on the tumultuous seas, but the daily shallop reports provided little cause for optimism. Two weeks passed and still the shallop was not ready. I have always struggled to wait patiently. The struggle grew daily as there was no definitive end in sight.

It eased the stress a little with the crew taking me, some of the other women, and the children to shore a few more times. After so many weeks of the constant rolling of the ship, walking along sandy beaches felt wonderful, even with the bracing wind turning my cheeks red. I considered it a sign of progress. I could tell that the trip ashore did much to refresh William's spirits as well. He told me, "I rather prefer viewing the ship from shore than the shore from ship." From the twinkle in his eyes as he spoke, I knew he was feeling more settled about our current circumstances.

~ ~ ~

Life aboard the ship settled into a new routine. Preparing meals and tending to daily necessities still consumed hours of each day, but now we either went to shore or relished the additional space available during the day with so many men off the ship. Carpenters worked on the shallop. Captain Standish marched an exploration party of sixteen men along the coast. Mr. Hopkins delighted in telling us stories comparing this new place to places he encountered on his previous visit to the New World.

I suspect it still sometimes bothered William that he did not explore the area with the younger men, but both Governor Carver and Mr. Bradford reminded him his service as our spiritual leader was too important to compromise his strength and health. I marveled at how patiently and graciously he accepted a role he hadn't sought out and at times must surely have wished he could set aside.

~ ~ ~

The second expedition explored on foot beyond the men who were reassembling the shallop, including Mr. White. While he was ashore, his young son Resolved, rushed up to tell me, "Mama says to come now. Now is the time."

I asked Dorothy to get hot water from the cook. Then I and several other women rushed to Susanna. Since this was not her first baby, it was only a few hours until she delivered a healthy baby boy.

When Mr. White returned from the exploration two days later, he announced the baby's name should be Peregrine, because he was the first child born in this New World, having come from another country. Susanna stayed in the tween deck, wrapped in layers of blankets and proudly showing off her newborn to anyone who wanted to admire his ruddy complexion and silky black hair.

~ ~ ~

Captain Standish was certain that on the second expedition they would find something if they explored long enough. On the ship he must have often been disappointed and frustrated with our men. Our people were farmers from rural England. Out of necessity, many had secured work in the textile factories in Holland, but none had any experience, or in all honesty, much interest, in sailing or military matters. I think our men were eager to prove they were worth more than just talking and praying. So, the hunting group that day was very focused as they wandered further down the shoreline to find a new spot to explore in hopes of bringing back something to show off.

The men returned from the expedition looking gaunt from the exertion, but also pleased with themselves. They discovered a large cast iron kettle which sat in the longboat as they gave their report. They were totally exhausted after two days of tromping through snow without proper protection from the cold. I peered over the railing to see the pot for myself. It looked like one I left behind in Scrooby and another left in Leyden. I wondered how one got here in this desolate place. As we took turns examining it, Captain Standish gave a report.

Kathryn Brewster Haueisen

Stephen Hopkins expanded after Standish finished because he was excited, recounting, "We saw five or six natives, like the ones I saw at Jamestown. We followed them for maybe ten miles before we lost them. We found several springs of fresh water, and we drank it with as much delight as ever we drank in all our lives. Then we came to a place where a house used to stand and found this here kettle. We also found a buried basket full of corn."

Mr. Bradford, too excited to wait his turn, interjected, "We shall be sure to pay the Indians for their corn, if ever we should meet up with them. And their kettle, as well, if we see them."

At least we had some corn to plant in the spring.

Chapter 19

December 12, 1620

On December 7, young Dorothy Bradford fell overboard to her death. I struggle to breathe even now as I think about it. Others have become seriously ill. Dear Lord, what is to become of us? I thought after arriving here the hardships would be only finding sufficient food and shelter.

I clung to the hope that once we reached land our situation would continue to improve, and it did in some ways, but we soon had other challenges to overcome. Five of our fellowship became gravely ill from food poisoning. They were so eager to dine on something fresh they indulged in clams, oysters and mussels they found on the beach. The men recovered and returned to exploring the area or working on the shallop. Poor Elinor Billington was sick several days, which afforded her mischievous boys new opportunities to stir up trouble.

The day her son Francis nearly set the barrel of gunpowder ablaze was still a popular topic of conversation whenever we had a lag in conversation over the winter. Most of the crew were no better than heathens, but the Lord used one of them save us all that day. It was his quick actions when he tamped out the sparks from the gun blast that saved us. Francis was bored and took his father's hunting gun when no one was looking. The thing was nearly as long as he was tall and he had no business fooling with it.

I should hope the blast of it that landed him on his fanny and the sparks in the barrel put some sense in him. But I rather doubt that it did. Poor Elinor. Though she is one of the Strangers, my heart goes out to her. No woman deserves all the trouble she gets from the men in her family.

Our progress in finding a suitable place to establish ourselves depended on finishing the work on the shallop. The men had explored all they could on foot in the bitter winter weather. By the end of our third full week at anchor, the carpenters finally finished reassembling the shallop. Twenty-four of our men, plus ten more of the crew, including Master Jones, set out again, this time taking both the longboat and our shallop. From the deck we watched them set out across the bay and then promptly turn back toward shore. The wind was so strong it hurt even to stand on the deck. I could only imagine how treacherous it must be for the men in the boats. I could see the spray of seawater on them, drenching their clothes.

Though we had come at last to the New World, I also came to a new place of despair. Of all the images I had about life in a wilderness, being trapped for months on a ship was not among them. I worried about wild animals—perhaps lions, or tigers, bears or wolves. I had heard stories about bears twice the size of a grown man lurking in the New World. I had heard of a man in England who was torn apart by a wolverine and shuddered to think such a thing might happen to someone among our fellowship.

What I did not envision was night after night listening to people coughing or retching from whatever illness plagued them. I had not imagined how crowded and foul would be our living accommodations. I did not foresee the bitter resentment the crew would have against us. And I certainly did not anticipate that I would send the Pecke children

Kathryn Brewster Haueisen

off to other families only to take on two more children that had been abandoned by total strangers.

William keeps urging me to be patient. I keep asking, "How long, O Lord. How long?" I had to be patient nearly a year with William in hiding. I've been trapped on this ship since July and it is now nearly January. Isn't that long enough?

And now many are succumbing to sickness and neither our dear Deacon Fuller nor the ship's Dr. Heale have proper medicine to help them. What a sorry state of affairs. How far I've fallen from my days of peace and prosperity at Scrooby Manor. Is this truly the will of God? Or the result of the overzealous imaginations of a few men with more passion than realistic perspectives of the situation?

It seemed each day someone else fell seriously sick from lack of fresh food. Those not yet sick, busied themselves tending to those who were. We still grieved over the death of Deacon Fuller's servant. How could we have known that turned out to be the prelude to a season of sickness. With each death my heart constricted a little more. Mr. Edward Thompson was the first to die after we anchored. He was the young servant to the White family, but his youth provided no protection against the hardships of weather and poor nutrition. Susanna grieved something fearsome. There she was, far away from home with little Resolved and now baby Peregrine, not even a month old yet. Her husband William was on another expedition when Edward died.

Susanna looked to me for comfort, but I was worn out with my own worries. Yet, I was bound by conscience to assist her as best I could. Her new baby had a powerful pull on my sympathy.

Each day delivered another tragedy until they stacked up around us like fire logs. Abandoned Jasper More, assigned to Governor Carver and Katherine, was only seven when he died a couple of days after the White's servant. Both his sisters died before the men finished our first shelter. Death always distresses me, but all the more when the Grim Reaper takes a child. What short, miserable lives they had. Taken away from their mother. Foisted on me and the others like so much extra baggage. Then three of them dead within weeks of arriving in the New

World. We desperately needed vegetables and berries, yet winter was hard on the land and there would be no green shoots to add to our diet for months.

Of all the deaths, the most unsettling one occurred the day after Jasper died. It was the 7th of December. The exploration party was away again, this time across the bay and determined to choose the location of our future settlement. I sat with William and the children, fascinated at my husband's ability to make up a story on the spur of the moment to entertain the children.

We all heard the commotion when a voice from above cried out, "Man Overboard! Man Overboard!" The boys popped up and headed to the ladder. I grabbed two of them by their shirts. At the same time William announced firmly, "No, you may *not* go up. We shall learn soon enough what happened. You would be in the way."

They grumbled and fussed but sat back down. The news shocked me. Mr. John Chilton, in his sixties, saw what happened. He wept openly as he descended the ladder slowly and approached us, shaking his head back and forth. His face was pale. He spoke softly, pausing between each word. "It . . . was . . . Dorothy . . . Bradford. She . . . was . . . looking . . . out across the bay." He stopped talking and dabbed at his eyes.

"Go on, man. What happened?" asked William.

"I suppose she hoped to see the expedition returning. I guess she leaned out too far. She. She. She went overboard."

I gasped.

Mr. Chilton put a hand on a beam to steady himself. "Sailors rushed to hand down the long-handled net. She latched on but lost her grip. A wave washed over her face. She spurted out salt water and coughed and reached for the pole again. But another wave pushed her away."

He could not continue, so William guessed, "And she went under?"

He nodded and found his voice again. "She went under three times . . . before she disappeared for good."

Kathryn Brewster Haueisen

The boys tucked themselves in around me, I guess knowing I needed the warmth of their young bodies to soften the blow. William started to speak, but I put my hand on his arm to stop him. I figured he would pull out another passage of scripture from his vast repertoire of memorized verses. I had no patience for it. Not right then. I was too angry at the senselessness of it. I wanted to yell and scream and hit something. *Why!?* Why three of the More children and now her? I could see I shocked William when I blurted out, "Not now, please, William. Not now. I cannot bear it. I prefer you take the children and leave me alone for once."

He nodded, gathered the children, and led them away. I wrapped my arms around my raised knees and let tears flow unabashed. My skirt was drenched before I ran out of tears. I had one bit of scripture of my own stuck in my head. It was one William spoke often when it was time to commit someone to the next life. I think he quotes from Lamentations. "The faithful love of the Lord never ends." I couldn't get the passage out of my head, but right along with it I kept thinking, *the Lord has a mighty strange way of showing love.*

And still the Grim Reaper was not done harvesting among us.

The next day Mr. Chilton followed Dorothy into the next life. The sickness did him in. Another widow and fatherless child. I couldn't keep from thinking, *Is this compulsion to establish a new colony truly worth the cost? Is God telling us we are worshipping incorrectly? Why are we finally here and having the worst time of the entire voyage?*

~ ~ ~

The next day the expedition party returned to the ship. We all gathered around them, eager to hear what they had to report. Mr. Bradford was as animated as the others, all talking at once, excited about the good news they brought. I heard William suck in all the breath he could contain and very slowly release it before leaving my side. William accepted his duty as our spiritual leader and stepped forward to inform Mr. Bradford about Dorothy.

I saw him put his hand on Mr. Bradford's shoulder and guide him away from the crowd. They disappeared down the ladder to the tween deck. William soon returned. "He wishes to be alone with his grief. I think it best we grant him that request as nothing any of us can do or say will bring her back to life."

We waited several hours. Then I solicited help from a couple of the other Leyden women to assemble a light supper for him. He sat as if in a trance. I could not be sure he even knew who we were.

We offered him the food, but he waved it away. He stayed like that for a couple of days. Then he resumed his work among us. He never spoke of her death again that I ever heard about. People speculated he was too distraught to speak of it. Governor Carver suggested perhaps he felt guilty for bringing her on the voyage. Whatever his reasons, he kept them to himself.

Chapter 20

December 28, 1620

> *Master Jones reports we were 66 days at sea! No wonder we are all so weary of this ship! But now the men have found a suitable place for our new settlement and can commence building shelter for us. To be off this large rolling ship will be a great joy. Two of the babies born on this floating frigid foul ship still live. One does not.*

It is strange how the events of life mingle our darkest hours with our strongest hopes. Master Jones' demeanor improved considerably after that day, though he was still crusty and stern on the subject of preserving his beer and other provisions for himself and his crew. We were able to make do with whatever our men could catch, trap or shoot and the few things left in the bottom of our own barrels.

Poor Elizabeth Hopkins, Susanna White and Mary Allerton got not a pinch of salt worth of compassion from the crew while enduring their birthing travails. At least Oceanus and Peregrine seem hearty enough. Poor, dear Mary though. She and Isaac buried a babe just last

February back in Leyden. Then here in this harbor she delivered a stillborn on the 22nd of this month. Her living children beg for her attention, but she is frozen in her grief. I wonder if she will survive the losses so close together.

Grief or no grief, we had to keep going. Master Jones had the crew pull up anchor and set out early the next morning, but the weather turned foul so he turned around and returned to the harbor. William continued to see the benefit of whatever happened, accepting each day with a patience that bordered on what seemed to me to be an utter lack of appreciation for the precarious nature of our situation. I struggled to match his calm lack of complaints.

When Master Jones finally considered it sufficiently safe enough to cross the bay, he instructed the crew to again pull up anchor and cross, at long last, to where we would establish Plimoth Plantation. We still lacked any adequate shelter, were coming to the end of our food rations, and faced a bitterly cold winter, with no evidence of spring. Nonetheless, I felt buoyant and hopeful. I could see where I would soon enough live on land again. That thought carried us all through the bleak mid-winter snow and ice.

English Master John Smith had already named this place Plimoth, a familiar name that warmed my heart. William was quick as a fox to point out this was where the Lord meant for us to be all along. I suspected he may have been correct but wished the Lord had not taken quit so long to bring us to it. We further gave it the grand name of Plantation because it would be a town reliant on itself for all we might need to survive, Plimoth Plantation would feed our bodies and our souls and we would all take part in working to build it.

The men began construction on the first common house. We soon removed a few of our things off the ship, which gladdened Master Jones considerably. Once anchored in the harbor, with the longboat and shallop ferrying people back and forth each day, spirits lifted tremendously. However, for each improvement to our situation, we met a counter circumstance of another death. Some succumbed to scurvy, some pneumonia. Others lived but were so worn down from the cold and limited portions of food that they were too weak to do any work.

By January the men had completed the first structure, our Common House. Some moved into it and settled the sickest nearest the large fireplace. I stayed aboard the ship with the other women and children; grateful for more room, crossing the bay each day with a few of the ship's crew. Only a half dozen of us were well enough to care for the many sick among us. Captain Standish, William and I, along with a few others, had to do everything for everyone. We fetched wood for the fire, stacking as much extra as we had time to collect in the Common House. The men searched for anything edible in the woods and caught a few fish. Efforts to hunt resulted in an occasional animal to roast.

I and the other women sat with the sick by day, spooning broth into their mouths and wiping their brows. I spent the first days in our new home changing sick people's foul clothes and doing all manner of other things I prefer to forget. Yet the memory of the smell stays with me all these years later.

The crew stopped mocking us once they also fell ill. The manner in how we tended to our sick fellowship was so different from the crew. We offered whatever tender mercies we could to our sick. It was not so among the crew. Whenever one of their own fell sick, they left the poor fellow to languish alone until his health returned or he died.

Mr. Bradford shook his head in distain. He continued to hope that as they observed the way we treated one another with Christian charity, it would turn their hearts slowly toward the Lord.

One day William and I tended to a sailor who was near death, he was so weak he could barely speak, but managed to say, "I now see how you show your love like Christians to one another; but we let one another lie and die like dogs. I know I am passing; will you please accept me and say over me the same things?"

How sad that the Lord must sometimes resort to tragedy to bring people together. Once Master Jones' cook, master gunner, boatswain, and several more of his crew were felled by the sickness, his heart softened. He slowed down pressuring us to finish building our shelters. As the cruel winter continued to challenge our progress, he conceded that he could not abandon us until the worst of the snow-filled days let up.

We were trying to build a storage lodge to get all our belongings off the *Mayflower*, yet digging and building in the frozen middle of winter was slow going. The ocean was also at its most dangerous at this time of year. The captain's conclusion to stay was no doubt equal parts compassion for us and concern about a shortage of crew to tackle the Atlantic Ocean in such weather.

~ ~ ~

One day while on the *Mayflower* moving some barrels around, we saw smoke rising from the shore. Our new common house was on fire! Mercifully the men on shore responded quickly, so that only the thatched roof burned. It didn't take long for the men to repair the damage. Praise the Lord for problems readily resolved.

Our hunters saw a few Indians in the distance occasionally. This was soon the topic around our breaking bread each evening. We worried what they might do to us if they knew we were all weak and so many of us were dying as each week went by. A plan was hatched to bury our recently passed by lantern light. The graves were shallow due to the frozen ground, and close beside each other to disguise the number so any enemies would not realize how decimated we were. I vowed to mound up dirt in the summer and plant native wildflowers over these graves as an atonement for not being able to properly bury them. At least now, on land, we could have a decent mourning time and funeral speeches. Forty-five of our fellowship passed to God those few snowy months before spring finally burst upon us. Captain Standish has suggested we prop up our dead men with muskets around the area and bury them later, a show of numbers to ward off any attacks.

Kathryn Brewster Haueisen

William responded with astonishment to that suggestion. He said that didn't show proper respect for the departed. Captain Standish countered that we must do what we could to protect the ones who yet lived. I knew William didn't approve, but he didn't press the matter further. Some of our men planned to shoot at the first signs of Indians, to let them know we were prepared to protect ourselves. Others thought we should wait to see how they might respond to us. We will never know if having some of the dead propped up with muskets helped us or not. I do know my dear husband said a few more prayers for them than he normally did, perhaps by way of an apology to their souls.

Our safety was much talked about in those early days. William admonished us to adopt the latter approach of not shooting aggressively at the very sight of an Indian. "We do not know their intention and it would surely bring more death upon us if we stir them to retaliation. I must remind you that Pastor Robinson urged us to live in peace among each other, Saints and Strangers, and among any we should encounter, to the extent it is possible to do so. Remember that we are here for our own freedom, freedom to worship as we know we are called to; let that be our main concern. We won't be guilty of not allowing others their own freedom to connect with God as they see fit."

Though some thought peace a poor substitute for a show of strength, none wished to go against my husband after witnessing him perform the vilest tasks imaginable to nurse the sick back to health. I admired his calm, and even more so his stern way of cajoling others to heed his council. It helped, too, that Governor Carver pointed out that while we had muskets against their arrows, they had many, many more warriors shooting arrows than we had men firing muskets. It was agreed that we not take any first steps at warring; using our guns only for defense so as to settle into this new land in the most peaceful way possible.

With spring's arrival we had many reasons to give thanks. Waterfowl, rabbits, beavers, fish and all manner of wildlife I had never seen before began to stir and our men were soon bringing in the bounty. This made for much improved diets. I longed for fruit and fresh vegetables, but the ample supply of cooked meat did much to enhance our spirits.

How I avoided the sickness that first winter I cannot explain. Perhaps it was the will of the Lord so that I might provide for the many who lost family in those early months. Gradually, we moved our things from the ship to the new cottages as more of us gained the strength to tug and roll and push the boxes and barrels. It was a joyous day when I left the stink of the ship for good.

No fond memories of that time occupy my thoughts, nor do I ever dream of those months confined there. I still sometimes dream about the manor in Scrooby or our home along the alley in Leyden. I have heard there are those who make their homes in boats moored to the docks along the canals in Amsterdam, but I cannot fathom feeling secure in a place that could sink!

~ ~ ~

Moving into our humble cottage was thrilling.

Compared to the confinement of the tween deck, and then living on top of one another in the Common House, it felt spacious. I could stretch my arms as far as they would go and not bump into someone. I could stand without latching onto someone or something to stay upright. I had a chair on which to sit.

Never before I had considered simply sitting on a chair a luxury; but months without doing so altered my perspective.

William had his favorite chair now as well. It had been in the hold of the ship for months, out of reach. Now he savored sitting in it while reading one of his many books. In spite of our limitations on what we could bring, he managed to have sufficient books to occupy him happily many mornings and evenings.

At first Mr. Bradford lived with us. His wit and intelligence eased some of William's sadness at not having his long talks with Pastor Robinson. It touched me how my husband both advised and served the younger man.

Chapter 21

March 2, 1621

I have not had time to make journal entries much of late. Mr. Bradford is gravely ill and Priscilla Mullins is orphaned, the only one of her family to still live. Apparently, the good Lord intends for me to be a substitute mother and friend to the growing list of widows, widowers and orphans.

The weather has turned mild during the days and those of us able to do work are setting about getting our seeds into the ground. Every waking minute is spoken for, yet how much more joyous is this tiredness at day's end than the relentless rolling smelly ship.

In March, we got to work preparing the soil for our first garden. It felt glorious to work the damp spring soil, to smell the rich loam, while listening to birds calling out from their perches nearby. The wind was still chilly, but in the warmth of the sun, it felt invigorating, like receiving the promise of better times to come.

At the start, being so few of us up to the rigors of establishing a garden, we shared one large plot. I enjoyed working with the other women while admiring the large fluffy clouds overhead. The bay water was calm, with only a few ripples. I worked with my legs bent on the ground, using my hands and a trowel to make furrows. Others came along behind me with the seeds.

The third or fourth day of our spring planting changed our whole lives, and probably saved our lives in the bargain.

The children were at the shore trying to catch eels. Our men stood nearby, conferring with Master Jones. I heard his gruff voice even from some distance. "I need to know when you will be fully off my ship! Me and me men need to set sail."

Their meeting was interrupted when Captain Standish pointed toward the top of the hill and yelled, "Look! There! See? One of them approaches!" Without thinking, he removed his musket from his shoulder and pointed it at the Indian.

The man stopped. As if planned, Mr. Winslow, on Captain Standish's left, and my husband on his right, both pushed his musket toward the ground. "He comes alone. See, he has his arms stretched out—empty. He means us no harm," assured Mr. Winslow.

My husband agreed, adding, "We must do whatever is feasible to maintain peace! Though they have not our sort of weapons, what they do have could easily end a life and we are too few to risk taunting them."

Captain Standish relaxed a bit but kept a tight grip on his musket. The Indian took a few tentative steps forward. Governor Carver pushed Mr. Bradford and Mr. Winslow forward toward him. "Go greet him. Hold your hands out as he does, to extend him a welcome."

I was as fascinated as I was nervous.

I looked to the shore and wondered if I should call the children to come to me. Or perhaps quietly walk to them and bring them back. Lacking any clarity on the best course of action, I froze where I was. I sat back on my haunches and waited.

Kathryn Brewster Haueisen

The Indian took a few steps closer and stopped. Mr. Winslow and Mr. Bradford took a few steps toward him, then stopped. Like some sort of awkward dance, the Indian would advance and stop. Our two men would mimic his movements.

No one spoke.

Even the birds seemed to sense something urgent was unfolding, for I no longer heard their chirping. When the three were perhaps the length of our long boat apart from one another, the Indian called out clear as a church bell. "Welcome, Englishmen."

My hand flew to my mouth and I gasped. **English!**

Our men gawked and turned toward us. "He speaks English!" exclaimed Mr. Bradford.

I had often wondered what it would be like when we should at last meet an Indian face to face. I never imagined one would approach us speaking English. His face was painted with black and red stripes. He wore a deerskin breechclout, leggings and shirt, and ankle-high moccasins. The three of them walked closer to where we worked in the garden.

Mr. Bradford stammered, "You, you speak English?"

"I know your tongue," the Indian confirmed. "Many others come—there," he said as he turned to pointed across the bay to the north. "They make trade with my people."

All garden work stopped. We stood, straining to hear what was happening. The children stood where they were and gaped. I signaled that I wanted them to stay where they were. Apparently, they understood for they sat on the ground, totally entranced by the scene playing out among the adults.

A breeze picked up, rustling enough leaves that I could not make out their words, I could see they were friendly toward one another. I felt my heart thumping. This first contact could go so many ways. Our safety, even our survival, depended on this going well.

After a few minutes the Indian went with our men to Mr. Hopkin's new cottage. I called for the children to come. They raced to the garden, bursting with questions I could not answer. We set aside the garden work and speculated about what was happening in that cottage.

Time moved slowly, it seemed hours, before the door opened.

Mr. Bradford emerged first. He was smiling. Then my husband. He too was smiling. Captain Standish emerged. He was not smiling, but his musket was back over his shoulder where it always was if he was not aiming it at something. Then I saw the Indian. He did not smile either, but he seemed pleased. The others came out one by one. They escorted the Indian back across the brook and into the treeline.

Observing us standing in a cluster staring at them, Mr. Bradford approached and gave us a report. "This Indian told us he is called Samoset and he has met others like us who have come here before to trade. That is how he can speak our language. He is the sagamore of his people."

We soon learned that meant he was their leader and that he was acquainted with another who once lived in London! An Indian who lived in London! William announced it must be another sign that we would succeed. I dared hope he spoke truthfully.

After months of worrying about what would happen if Indians attacked us, here came one alone speaking English. It jolted me hearing one who looked so different speaking familiar words.

Perhaps things would work out for us after all.

~ ~ ~

By March we had our Common House completely finished. This grand structure doubled as a place for those recuperating from the ravages of the winter and our meeting and worship area. Plus, the men had built the first seven cottages. The settlement plan had been nineteen homes, one for each family. That plan didn't include so many dying or being too weak to help build their homes. We settled for what we had and were plenty grateful for it. Reality has a way of altering the best of plans.

Kathryn Brewster Haueisen

Two months earlier I still lived on the ship surrounded by other people. The only space we had for living included piles of everyone's clothes and bedding, ceaseless conversations, the unpredictable pitching of the ship, the two dogs, chickens, piglets and our goats. Compared to all that, what we had by March seemed luxurious.

Our progress was evident in many small ways. The general tone of conversations changed from chronic complaints and laments to one of optimism, anticipation and plans for the future with liberal tangents on the nature of Indians and much speculation on how they lived.

The children whined less once they were free to move about in the fresh air.

Master Jones even occasionally complimented us on our industriousness.

The chickens strutted about their new yards cackling and flapping their wings and gifting us with fresh eggs now and then. The pigs roamed through the woods digging and finding their own food. They could do this and need very little care other than shelter during bad weather until we decided it was time to butcher one and make good use of every part of it in some way. We wanted to wait until we were sure the sows were giving birth before deciding which pig would go first.

We had planted our first crops. Each family took in one or more of those who had no other family. Our home included me and William, our sons, Richard More, and Mr. Bradford. Nearly every family had buried at least one family member. The rigors of the crossing melded us into one large family. Tragedy wiped away many of the differences we initially let divide us. They no longer seemed that important. We needed one another too much.

~ ~ ~

Samoset returned in a few days with a young man who looked to be about the age of Jonathan. Seeing him made the longing for my son swell until I thought I might burst with the ache of it. This Indian was tall and lean. Speaking remarkably good English, he explained how an earlier Englishman kidnapped him and two dozen more six years earlier. He ended up living in London. Once he spoke good English, he proposed to the man where he lived that he could return to his home and help white men make trade with his people.

I was astonished. We all were. An Indian who spoke English as well as any of us, standing before us offering to help us communicate with other Indians. I saw that William was right in believing this must be part of the Lord's plan for us. He called himself Tisquantum but seemed not to mind that we called him Squanto.

Still astonished at this turn of events, I and the other women left the men to further ply the Indian with questions. We needed to prepare the next meal. Though we had our individual cottages, we still often ate together in the Common House to share both the labor and the food.

Deacon Fuller followed us.

He served as our doctor, as well as a deacon in our fellowship. Those who survived the season of sickness did so largely due to his diligent care for them. Deacon Fuller was much respected and loved. He commenced helping us put together a meal from the sparse ingredients we had to offer our first guests. A rare gesture for a man.

I was not accustomed to help with cooking tasks from a man. Perhaps Deacon Fuller regretted insisting that his wife Bridget remain in Leyden. Or, more likely, he was worried about our safety and feigned wanting to help as his gentle way of being with us without alarming us. Though the situation seemed to unfold peacefully enough, none of us were totally convinced we might not still be in danger. Perhaps the two Indians had come only to give an accurate account of our severe situation to their warriors. Only Mr. Hopkins had any experience with the ways of these strange looking people. He and Captain Standish repeatedly warned us to be alert and ready to lock up the women and children and send men with weapons out to defend us.

Kathryn Brewster Haueisen

Whatever Deacon Fuller's reasons, I was both grateful and confused that a man should take time to help. But help he did, and thanks to him, all was ready when our two peculiar visitors came to share a meal.

If this was truly the Lord's doing, it is most certainly true the Lord works in mysterious ways. I felt hopeful and peaceful as I reflected on how fortunate we were to have these English-speaking Indians come offering help. I began to think Mr. Hopkins and Captain Standish were secretly hoping for any indication of trouble so they could justify using their weapons for more than hunting game and waterfowl. I was stunned with what our Indian guests told us as we shared this meal together.

"My people lived here," Squanto announced after he wiped his hand over his mouth to clear away the gravy that lingered there.

"What do you mean?" asked Mr. Hopkins. "We have not seen any others of your kind here."

He explained that while he was in London, the Great Dying called on the very place we sat sharing a meal. All the people either died or left. And now we established our new plantation here. The phrase "life after death" kept rolling through my head.

"I came back with an English explorer. We came down this way from far away." He pointed north. "So much death. Bodies across the beaches. Villages empty. All my people—gone." He shrugged his shoulders and stared at the dirt floor, with his fists clenched at his sides.

The silence that followed was eerie. Unnatural. Like the first hours after a storm when even the birds stop singing. I felt heavy with sorrow for this young man's loss. What if something like that happened to Jonathan? What would he have done? Would he have had this young man's resourcefulness to apply himself to a new way to survive?

It was such a tug on my emotions. I felt sorry for his plight; but equally grateful to be done with that torturous trip and settling into our new plantation. Looking out across the bay at the spectacular sunrises, the aroma of the sea, and birds gracefully gliding overhead—it was hard to fathom the depths of suffering that had happened right where I stood.

Learning Squanto's story reminded me to savor the sweet moments of life, for we certainly experience enough sour ones. Day by day this little area along the bay looked more like a village and less like a wilderness. But finding out we had a home because strangers we would never know died or abandoned their homes, cast a shadow over the situation. That is the trouble with trauma. It seems wrong to be happy in the face of other people's suffering. Yet, it seems equally wrong, ungrateful, not to appreciate and rejoice over good fortune. Sorrow and joy seem always to be braided together like the strands of a rope.

I felt unsettled thinking about it, the way I felt when I was large with Jonathan before he was born. My cousin wept bitter tears when her first baby died at birth. If I rejoiced for my baby, I felt callous toward my cousin's loss. If I grieved with her for her loss, I felt ungrateful for all I had.

William tried to make sense of how death and life are braided together in the long chord of life. How the death of one situation prepares for the way for another situation to spring forth. Just as in the garden, when I work dead leaves into the soil to nurture the new plants.

Yes. Of course. But this young Indian's people were not dead leaves. Admittedly, they looked nothing like us; not in dress, nor appearance, nor actions. Yet, I could not refrain from comparing Squanto to Jonathan. If they knew one another, would they become friends? Might they someday meet? I clung to the hope that any day we would see a ship sailing across the bay bringing more of our Leyden fellowship to us. Of course, they had no way to know exactly where we were or even if we made it alive. Soon the *Mayflower* would carry them the news and we could expect some sweet reunions.

But for now, there was no ship, only these strange men among us, inquiring about our plans and offering to show us a better way to care for ourselves here.

At worship the next Sabbath William compared Squanto's story to Joseph. "Joseph's brothers sold him into slavery because they were

Kathryn Brewster Haueisen

jealous of him. God used that to place Joseph in Egypt when the famine came. He was there to aid his brothers, even though they betrayed him. See how the Lord continues to use events to favor those it pleases Him to bless. An Englishman took this Indian to Europe where he ended up in London. There he learned English. Now he is here and he can help us and his own people in many ways. The Lord has surely shown his favor upon us."

All the while, Captain Standish stood on alert near the back with his musket by his side glancing about for anyone sneaking up on us. It occurred to me that William talked about the ideal while Captain Standish focused on the probable. Which man had the right approach? After all, how do we know that an Indian might not kidnap our children to retaliate?

William preached the need for peace and friendship as the path to security in the future. Captain Standish constantly alerted us to danger 'til was a wonder any of us slept a wink. Others, Governor Carver, Mr. Bradford, Deacon Fuller, even Mr. Hopkins, struggled to find a way to agree with both points of view. I had no experience, good or ill, with any Indian. I could not decide who spoke more rightly.

Enriching these sermons and discussion of safety, Samoset and Squanto were frequent visitors; apparently relishing the opportunity to share a meal with us. Neither seemed terribly threatening. Rather, they both reminded me of the many other men I knew who loved to eat whatever women put in front of them. Though, they did look peculiar with clothing made from deer hides, their golden-bronze skin, long, straight black hair, and eyes as dark as coal.

Looking at them served as a constant reminder we were no longer in England or the Lowlands. I wondered if we looked as strange to the Dutch when we immigrated there as these two looked to me now. And, I suppose, we must look strange to them as well. I had never thought about it much, but it is amazing how different we can be from one another and still have so much in common. We all have people we claim as family and community. We all have to have food, and shelter, and some sort of clothing; most of all, the smiles we exchanged gave the same message of warmth.

Another thing that transpired at this meal felt quite familiar. The men did all the talking. I wondered what the Indian women were like, and if I should soon have a chance to meet one. Our women did the cooking, fetching this and that, and keeping the children from interrupting. Though I was curious to know more about how their women lived, I would not learn about it that spring. I resigned myself to being grateful these first encounter had been peaceful.

Squanto's ability to speak to our men in English continued to amaze me. I tried to imagine him walking along the busy streets of London. I suppose whoever he lived with may have insisted he wear more proper attire, but even so, he would surely stand out. The combination of his bronze skin, long, straight black hair, and his height would make it impossible for him to blend in among the men of London. Observing him with Samoset, talking to us in our own language, was a refreshing mix of surprise and relief after ten years surrounded by the Dutch tongue. They switched to their own language several times, gesturing and laughing. Were the making fun of us? We had no way of knowing. That part was like being back in Leyden when the Dutch moved from English back to Dutch and I was left out of the conversation.

From his earlier adventures in the New World, Mr. Hopkins knew a few of the Indians' ways but, as he explained, the Indians he met before spoke a different language than these two. He was powerless to interpret for us. We had to trust that while they were laughing, they meant us no harm. Yet, it was disconcerting to realize they could be plotting to murder us all on the spot and we would not know it from their talk.

When they switched back to English, they announced that their great leader wanted to meet us. Having two English-speaking Indians announce something so grand never occurred to me.

Squanto explained they call their king Massasoit, and he ruled over thousands of Indians. ***Thousands!***

Kathryn Brewster Haueisen

In all the months our men had been exploring and hunting, they had never seen more than a few dozen, and none up close until these two came to us. The men had seen or heard evidence of perhaps a hundred or so. But thousands? Our weapons would be of little use if they decided they didn't want us here.

After hearing about Squanto's kidnapping and their Great Sickness, I worried they might want to chase us all back on the ship that still bobbed in the bay.

Or worse.

I shuddered thinking about what worse might be. It made my blood run cold. I could feel fear moving up my spine and clutching at my stomach. I wanted to believe we were safe, but remnants of panic tugged at me even as I observed them gobbling down everything in sight.

I hoped Captain Standish was up to the challenge of protecting us, but it didn't seem likely we would be prepared for an attack considering how outnumbered we were. I hoped it was a good sign this king of theirs sent messengers rather than warriors. But what if this was some sort of a trick? Pretend to be friendly to get close enough to see for themselves how we fared.

When William told me of the plans for the next meeting, I questioned him hoping he would be able to calm my fear. "Their king will come here?! Is that wise? Would it not be better if a few of our men went to him?" He chastised me for having so little faith. I didn't see it as a lack of faith, only a presence of possibility for an attack and the need to be prepared.

I couldn't stem the tide of images of bloody, mutilated women and children that marched through my mind. I had a foreboding flashback of panic to the day the magistrates came looking for William; and the night the ship nearly capsized. I decided I needed to hold my fears in silence.

We might all be bludgeoned to death in our sleep, but Standish was well aware of this and eager to protect us.

Would meeting their leader prove a solution to our struggles? Or would this be the fatal event that brought an end to this grand experiment to establish our own new home?

"Mary, they too have suffered terribly. The Indians assure us, they want only peace."

More than ever before, I prayed what William said was true.

Kathryn Brewster Haueisen

Chapter 22

March 27, 1621

Though I sometimes wish he would speak about it less frequently, after the recent turn of events I have to concede that William is right to have this total trust in the Lord. If anyone had suggested back in Leyden that we would survive a mid-crossing gale of some kind to reach the New World and be approached by Indians who speak English, and that their great kind leader would offer to establish a treaty with us, I would have wondered if that person was drunk. Though of course the Indians are not Christian, they seem to want to make a good effort to be at peace with us. I begin to see the possibility of a wonderful future for all of us.

A day in late March, five days after Samoset brought Squanto for the long meeting and meal with us, proved a pivotal day in our community's history. I was working with the others in our garden, stopping often to wipe sweat from my brow. Governor Carver worked with us to expedite our progress, stopping every few minutes to do the same. He sat down on the ground where he took off his coat and dabbed at the back of his neck with a damp cloth.

While we labored in the garden, Master Jones supervised his crew tending to last tasks required to sail for England. They had labored many days hauling small boulders and bags of sand to the ship to replace the weight of all our things. The investors no doubt expected him to return with a ship full of dried fish, beaver pelts or other things they could convert to cash, not rocks and sand. But then, the investors didn't yet know of the unfavorable conditions that greeted us. We considered it providence to have enough of us alive to finish a few shelters and get seeds in the ground for the future. How easy it is for men of means to sit in the pubs and dream up marvelous schemes and how difficult it is for we who dig in the dirt and cut down the timber to make their dreams reality.

I inspected the new shoots poking out of the ground from our work of a few weeks ago and was pleased at what I saw. Today we were using a new technique for the next batch of seeds. Squanto had shown us how to fertilize the ground with dead fish. When I heard that, I thought he mocked us. But he was serious and worked a few holes until we understood. He said that at this time of year there were so many herring in the brook even a child could catch a few. He showed us how to place a fish at the bottom of a hole, then a little dirt and then a kernel of corn, more dirt, then the seeds for beans and squash. That is not how I gardened back in England or Leyden. But then, I had to keep reminding myself, I no longer lived in either of those places.

The house builders were still hard at work building the next cottage in our expanding plantation colony. As hungry for profits as the investors were, they did allow that we could work one day in seven on our own needs. The rest of our labor went to pay them back for financing our voyage and establishing our own free community; though no one was here to keep an eye on what we did, we wanted to pay off our debt and be free of them so we did not shirk our duty to the contract we signed with the Adventurers. Eventually we would have to

Kathryn Brewster Haueisen

make an accounting, but until another ship came bringing inspectors, we applied our efforts in equal measure to establishing our own structures and looking for ways to pay off our debt.

I longed for each family to have its own cottage after so many months cooped up together, but sharing a cottage was still much better that trying to establish any privacy in the tween deck. Once everyone had their own private cottage, life would be even better. That was the hope that drove us all to work each day. William encouraged me to appreciate how much better things were already. We had more food. We had the sun by day and fires in our fireplaces by night. At times I found his incessant positive outlook irritating; but I didn't feel better if I indulged in fuming or fretting. Nor did I truly want him to change his outlook.

Captain Standish urged us to fortify our cultivated area. He continued to warn us about potential attacks from Indians. Even if no Indians attacked, wild animals threatened to destroy our crops and we knew we had to protect them by any means available. So, in addition to all the other urgent work, building a blockade around our cottages occupied the efforts of some. By the end of March the number of men strong enough for such arduous work numbered not even two dozen.

We kept the sickest together in one building, still in the main Common House. This made it easier for us to care for them, and we hoped, perhaps, being near the fire and food might speed their recovery. Mercifully, by the ending of March, the death toll had slowed considerably. Praise the Lord for that! Some of the sick were starting to feel better. I attribute that to better lodging, improved weather and more options for food now that we could add sprigs of wild greens to the game animals.

We were all thus engaged in our various tasks when Squanto approached to inform Governor Carver their king and his brother were waiting at the top of the hill. With some effort, being quite tired from his work in the garden, Governor Carver got to his feet. With his hand across his forehead to shield the bright sun from his eyes, he looked where Squanto pointed. I looked too.

I dropped my trowel and gasped. There stood perhaps fifty or more Indians, all wearing deer skin clothes, beads, feathers, braids and other things that made them a most colorful sight.

I was gawking at them when William dashed over to implore all the women to gather the children and retreat to our cottages. "Stay there until we come to tell you it is safe to come out. Squanto says their king wants to meet with us, but we do not know how it will go."

I felt vindicated as I gathered the children. Perhaps I had good reason to be concerned if now even William, always seeing the good in others and some benefit in any situation, seemed to be concerned about our safety.

What happened next became one of those pivotal, life-altering events one never forgets. The sort of thing in which we remember with great detail exactly where we were and who we were with at the time. Like the day I learned Queen Elizabeth died.

I gathered the children, then went to our cottage door, straining to hear what Squanto and Samoset were saying. Their king proposed an exchange. He would send six of his men to our settlement as a sign of good faith. In exchange, he expected us to send one of our men to him, as evidence we also wanted peace. Squanto and Samoset were sent to escort one of ours to their king. True to his word, six of the Indians were slowly making their way down the hill, escorted by another Indian I presumed must be one of their leaders, since his clothing was more densely adorned with beads than that of the others.

At the very top of the hill one other Indian stood out among the rest. He wore even more necklaces and had an enormous yellow feather stuck in a band wrapped around his head. He stood with his arms crossed, staring straight ahead, out toward the horizon.

Mr. Winslow volunteered to go. Squanto and Samoset escorted him up the hill to present him to their king and the Indian standing next to him. I learned that was their king's brother. Mr. Winslow went armed only with some beads, knives and a copper chain to present to their king as a gesture of friendship. During all this, the two kings stood tall and silent, arms crossed across their chests. They reminded me of cats

Kathryn Brewster Haueisen

waiting to pounce on a mouse. Perhaps it was just the uncertainty; they could be friends or they could be setting us up for an attack. As if to echo my thoughts William called out to Squanto, Samoset and Mr. Winslow as they crossed the brook and made their way toward the foot of the hill, "Assure them that we seek peace."

Squanto cupped his hands, and shouted back to William, "He also wants peace. No war with the English."

When our man met the Indians at the foot of the hill, everyone stretched out their arms and extended open hands, confirming they did not plan to harm Mr. Winslow. I breathed a little better seeing that. The six exchange Indians then followed Squanto back toward our village, as Mr. Winslow went further up the hill.

About halfway up the hill, Mr. Winslow turned to look at us. I couldn't see his face very well from so far away. I imagine he was taking one long, good look at us, in case it should prove to be his last one. Admiration for his courage flooded me with gratitude. I felt my throat tighten and tears forming.

Still peeking from the door of my cottage, I watched Squanto approaching with the six Indians. Several of our men escorted the six Indians into the Common House. With the exchange completed, it was time for the rest of the Englishmen and Indians to meet.

~ ~ ~

I know what happened next because I defied my husband. Rather than stay inside the cottage, I decided to walk with the children behind other cottages, easing our way to where we could see, and I hoped hear, what was happening. I held my finger to my lips and crouched down, signaling for them to do the same.

My fear of some future rebuke from William was no match for my present desperate need to know for myself what was happening. I was certain my future depended on what transpired over these next few moments and finding out for myself demanded my full attention.

The king with the yellow feather, and perhaps two dozen of his men, approached the brook a few tentative steps at a time, stopping a few yards short of the water. The other one had returned to the top of the hill where he watched with the rest of the Indians, Samoset and Mr. Winslow.

Led by Governor Carver and Captain Standish, our men walked slowly toward the brook, stopping an equal distance from the water on their side as the Indians had on the other side. Using Squanto to interpret, the men sent messages back and forth. I could see William whispering something to Captain Standish and Governor Carver, but from where we hid, I could hear nothing. Squanto waded back and forth many times delivering messages.

Each time he did so, the Indians and our men edged a little closer to the brook, until they were inches from the gently flowing water. I was so proud of Governor Carver. He stood straight, head held high, his empty hands held out as a gesture of good will. William was right behind him, with one hand gently resting on the governor's shoulder, I suppose to encourage him. Our young friend Mr. Bradford stood erect on his other side. Captain Standish and Mr. Hopkins were right behind them. Governor Carver nodded his head up and down quickly to greet the Indian king.

In response the king nodded back and spoke. I learned later he said, "*Taniska. Aquene,*" which meant Welcome. Peace. The Indians carried no weapons, but several of our men had their muskets with them, pointed down toward ground, but ready if needed. That reassured me a bit, but I still held my breath waiting to see what would happen next. I could feel the tension.

I wondered if perhaps there were many more Indians just over the crest of the hill, out of sight, with arrows ready to charge down the hill and overcome us all in a matter of minutes. We had all heard tales like this, rumors about other settlements. I could never truly relax in our new home.

Kathryn Brewster Haueisen

Finally, the great Indian king and about twenty of his men stepped into the brook and splashed to our side. Our men backed up to make room. Then, with Squanto still explaining what each leader was saying, all of them, perhaps forty, led by Governor Carver, slowly marched toward the main street of our settlement. I let out a long breath of relief, and just as quickly panicked for a different reason. I imagined the tongue-lashing I would receive if William spotted us.

As they paraded slowly down the street between our row of cottages, the children and I rushed back to our home on the back side of the row. Only then did I realize that I was trapped. The only door into our cottage was on the street side, where the men were slowly walking and talking. They would soon go right past our small house and William would certainly see us if I tried to get to the door right now. Instead, I set the children to work behind the cottage, picking up small tree branches blown into the yard by an earlier storm. We shared one large community garden, but each cottage also had space for a small area for a few vegetables and herbs. Having the children stack the branches kept the children busy and I always needed more kindling. It also gave me an excuse to be outside of the cottage if I were caught.

My heart raced and I felt jittery. I didn't like being deceitful or dishonest with William. Yet, sometimes, if his expectations seemed unreasonable and I had no way to alter the traditions that dictate married life, I did little acts of defiance to gain some sense of influence in my otherwise restricted life. Though I love William, I didn't always appreciate how he, like all men, assumed I wanted to do his bidding and follow his lead without question.

At the moment, I wanted to see this peculiar parade that was passing by just a few feet away but was afraid to watch. My thoughts also wandered to how poor Mr. Winslow was faring. If he came through his time with the Indians alive, it was futile fretting about him. If he did not, that would signal troubles that could mean death for us all.

I was praying we would all still be alive when the sun set.

Suddenly, I heard William calling my name. Using my strongest mother voice, I told the children to stay where they were. I cautiously moved around the corner of the cottage, toward the sound of William's voice. He looked surprised to see me outside, so I rushed to explain before he could say a thing. "The children were restless. They are behind the cottage gathering kindling. Restless children need a task to occupy their energy."

He nodded in agreement before he spoke. "Mary! This is truly a day the Lord has made and we will soon be rejoicing in it. We will soon sit to discuss by what terms we shall dwell together in this land. But first, Governor Carver has suggested we have a celebration parade. You may bring the children to watch."

Relief washed over me like a waterfall. I rushed to grab the children and we arranged ourselves in front of our cottage. True to his account, the men lined up, four or five abreast, with two of our men on either side of their four men. Some of the Indians beat on small drums they carried. Others played something like a flute. Our men lacked such instruments, so instead marched to the beat of the Indian music, swinging their arms back and forth. Most of the men had set their muskets aside, but a few, including Captain Standish of course, carried theirs over their shoulder.

It was a glorious sight! I realized I was tapping my feet as if marching right along with them. Love, Wrestling and Richard More giggled and squealed with delight, clapping and jumping up and down. It did my heart good to see them happy again. Only a few weeks earlier we'd had to bury Richard's little sister, Mary. His brothers died also. Such a sad situation for children who had no say in how the adults who brought them into this world decided their fate. But now, Richard was laughing and the sound of it was as thrilling to me as all the rest of the excitement that surrounded us.

A couple of times I had to grab the boys to keep them from dashing away to join the parade. I realized then that they had never seen anything quite like this and it thrilled them. I noticed a few of the Indians twitching their lips to contain laughing at the boys. That gave me hope; they thought our boys were adorable. This was a wonderful sign for a good future.

Kathryn Brewster Haueisen

They stopped abruptly in front of Mr. Hopkins' cottage. The Indian king and perhaps a half dozen of his men followed Governor Carver inside. William and another half dozen of our men followed. The rest stood outside the door seeming to show off drums or muskets or whatever they had to each other. That cabin must have been stuffed full with all those men inside.

I ushered the children back in our cottage. Soon Elizabeth Winslow knocked on my door saying, "I cannot bear one more minute of waiting alone to learn the fate of my husband!" She crossed the room, into my open arms.

I was still hugging her when William appeared. "Mary, where is our pillow you brought from Scrooby? We have no throne for our distinguished king guest. I told Governor Carver about the silk pillow you refused to leave behind. We concur it would be the most suitable seat we could offer him."

I knew exactly where it was. The only storage space in the entire cottage was the wooden trunk we brought over from Leyden. I retrieved the pillow and handed it to William. I hugged it for a moment, hoping William might invite me to join him when he returned to Mr. Hopkins' cottage. That was foolish of me. Of course, a woman was neither expected nor welcome at such an important conference.

They stayed in Mr. Hopkin's cottage all afternoon.

Occasionally someone would come out to ask me or someone else to send in more food or drink. We asked what was happening, but the only news we got was that things were progressing well. It was maddening. I wondered if this was how a husband felt when he was destined to pace while other women assisted his wife in bringing forth a baby. I didn't pace, but neither did I accomplish anything. I tried to focus on mending, but found I was doing it all wrong and finally set it aside, realizing I was only making more work for myself. I took the children to the community garden to check on the progress of our planting efforts. We went down to the shoreline and looked for eels to catch.

Finally, as the sun was slipping away for the day, they emerged. Everyone was smiling or nodding their heads or both. Once the Indians left, William settled into his chair and laughed at my expression. "Yes, yes, I will tell you. We have come to an agreeable understanding. We shall ratify our agreement after their king has a chance to meet with his council, some two days' walk away. For now, Squanto is taking their six men back to the top of the hill. Samoset is bringing Mr. Winslow back to us. They will camp in the woods tonight and start for home tomorrow."

And that is how we came to have an agreement between our two peoples. In essence, the men all agreed that if any of either party were in trouble, the other party would come to help. The Massasoit and Governor Carver further agreed that should any of his people injure or do hurt to any of our people; we could determine the proper punishment, so long as we agreed to the same conditions if one of our men brought harm to any of his people. William said everyone agreed that was fair.

William reported the part of the negotiations that took the longest to work out was about weapons.

Some thought we must agree that men would go unarmed to call on the other party. Some of our men said that was too risky. "When the talk turned to weapons, some of our men talked so fast Squanto could not translate. I believe that was their intent. Their leader wanted us to agree that when any of them came to us, they should leave their bows and arrows behind them. That, of course, was agreeable to our side. It was the reciprocal expectation that some objected on the grounds we could not be certain they would not ambush us.

"Our young Mr. Bradford eventually got everyone to agree to that point. Things went smoothly after that. We assured their leader that our King James would esteem him as a friend and ally. He seemed pleased with that and we concluded our business shortly after that."

Kathryn Brewster Haueisen

Chapter 23

April 2, 1621

The new plants in the garden give reason for hope. The air is warming and full of the sounds of birds cooing and calling. Each day we make more progress on the cottages and other buildings we need to have to transform this place into our home. I feel as lighthearted as I have in months, perhaps years. We still face death and struggles, but the load is so much lighter now.

Mostly, I am grateful to return to the more rural and serene life I once knew in England.

Master Jones is pressuring us to settle affairs to the point he can leave. We go as fast as we can!

I felt safer knowing we had such an agreement with our Indian neighbors. Both Master Jones and Mr. Hopkins assured us this was an extremely fortuitous outcome. The next day I felt a little feverish and achy. I was obliged to rest several times during the day and moved about more slowly than usual. Perhaps it was my turn for others to care for me. Deacon Fuller suggested that with a treaty between us and the

Indians, all the anxieties of the past few months were clamoring for release at once. Perhaps my malnourished body was reacting to months of deprivations. His recommendation was simply to tell me, "You have had too much to do for so many in our fellowship. I think what you most need now is rest."

All well and good and easier for a man to obtain than me. As long as I could stand, others expected me to make food appear as regular as the sun coming up in the morning. More than a minuscule amount of rest was not going to happen if we were going to eat. Still, with the worries about the Indians resolved, the next night I did sleep better and felt considerably more hopeful. I noted a lightness to the mood throughout our fellowship that I had not observed before the afternoon of the treaty. There was a collective sense of hope.

We worked with more vigor and good cheer as we returned our attention to our most pressing needs: food, more housing and a palisade around our entire plantation.

Everyone who had the strength to stand upright worked on one task or another. The younger and stronger men felled trees for fuel and to make into clapboards for the homes. It was thrilling to watch men make planks from the tree trunks, skimming their axes along the bark once a tree was down. They would all work on a new cottage until it was done with openings left along one wall for a window and door. When finished, they moved on to build another cottage, while others put a thatched roof on the one just completed. Each cottage took weeks to finish, yet with work every day we would soon have a cottage for every family and I would have our own cottage finally as simply the Brewster House.

The weeks passed with all of us busy and happy. Being older, my husband and Governor Carver worked with us in the garden instead of with the heavy trees and building tools. By April the hot afternoon sun, combined with such hard work, rendered me exhausted. I could see that Governor Carver was also affected from the exertion. He paused often to rest with his hands propped on top of his hoe. He stood there

Kathryn Brewster Haueisen

with sweat dripping down his face, struggling to take in long, deep breaths.

One afternoon he excused himself to retreat to his cottage for something to drink. When he didn't return after some time, William went to check on him. He returned soon to report, "I thought perhaps he was sleeping, a mid-day nap I would most certainly endorse. I called his name but got no answer. When I tapped his shoulder, I knew he would never awaken from this nap."

No one spoke, but Elizabeth Hopkins caught his wife Katherine before she collapsed to the ground. Katherine sobbed as Elinor, Susanna and I formed a circle of sisterhood around her. Soon the men stopped their work and came running to see what caused this sudden outburst. Everyone began talking all at once. We stood that way for some time, the women trying desperately to console Katherine and the men all putting forth their ideas about what happened to her husband and what we should do next. He had been a wonderful governor; we lost a friend and a leader. Finally, Elizabeth hooked her arm through the crook of Katherine's arm and gently guided her into their cottage. As they left us, William suggested the rest of us move into the Common House, out of the hot sun. Once we were seated, he took his customary place in front of us.

"A hard blow to be sure is the death of this fine man. Yet, even as we grieve, we also give thanks for his witness and leadership among us. We have him to thank for this treaty of peace completed just three weeks ago. I shall miss him as much as I already miss my friend and our pastor, John Robinson. I shall write to inform our Leyden fellowship of this, for now we must give the good governor a proper Christian burial and funeral. We must also offer what tender mercies we can to poor Katherine. She has no children to comfort her and is so far removed from her dear sister Bridget back in Leyden."

We agreed on the details for this special burial and then turned to another important matter.

Who would govern us now?

The men discussed the matter while the women waited for their decision. Some suggested Mr. Winslow since he had shown such bravery in going with the Indians before we were convinced the Indians truly did want only peace between our people. Others put forth Mr. Bradford's name. When William put the question to him if he would be willing to serve us in such a manner, he responded in his typical bold, yet modest way. "Should all of my dearest friends entrust me with this charge, I should humbly, trusting the Lord to guide and direct my ways, agree to accept."

We were soon back to our tasks. The death of our governor and the appointment of a new one couldn't long disrupt our labor. The need for food and shelter caused us to abandon the traditional period of grieving we might have honored back in Europe.

Our need to console Katherine lasted only a few days beyond the day we buried Governor Carver. I believe the poor woman died from a broken heart, what with her two children and now her husband all dead. I think the thought of going on alone in this strange new place broke her heart.

The death of these good souls distressed me more than most. Katherine was my constant reminder of her sister, Bridget, my dearest friend in Leyden. She and I had shared stories about Bridget often. Whenever we did, I could pretend Bridget was close by, merely in another cottage or just down the street, and not all way back across the ocean. Again, I wondered if we were truly following the will of God or only the exotic plans of restless husbands.

One of our new governor's first official tasks was to write Pastor Robinson with an account of the many deaths we suffered, including that of his own sister-in-law. William had offered to write the message, but readily agreed it was more appropriate for Governor Bradford to do so. He then suggested to William that perhaps I should write something to Bridget. When William proposed the idea, I shied away. I didn't have his eloquent way with words and couldn't fathom what I might write that could possibly ease her heartache at the death of her sister.

Kathryn Brewster Haueisen

I should have anticipated that it would eventually come about that I end up doing it. I never did have any success resisting William's plans. His final plea was, "Mary, you alone will be able to summon forth the words that will ease our sister Bridget's sorrow. I suggest you spend a day thinking what you would say to her if you were with her in Leyden, and then write that the next day. The matter is urgent. Master Jones is determined to sail back any day now."

This led to several days of my composing the letter in my head. I thought. I wandered back and forth along the shore the rest of that day. Some of the time I looked down at the clam shells beneath me. Other times I stared out across the bay, hoping against any hope that if I looked long enough, I would see the land we left over the edge of the horizon. The next morning I wrote:

My dearest friend Bridget –

> *I promise you that what I write to you now causes me as much pain as I fear it will bring you when you read these words. As you are reading this, I imagine that your husband is reading another letter from Governor Bradford. Yes, young William Bradford is now our governor, for Governor Carver, may God rest his soul in eternal peace, died from what we believe was heat stroke early in April. This is the news that Governor Bradford must convey to your husband, and through him, the rest of our fellowship.*
>
> *It falls to me to inform you that not long after after Governor Carver succumbed to the ravishes of our situation, your dearest sister Katherine joined him in death.*

The stains you see here are my tears as I write you this news. I treasure the friendship I forged with Katherine as much as our friendship. This voyage has not treated any of us kindly. Too many are now buried in this strange place. The lack of privacy, and the resulting lack of properly caring for ourselves, along with nearly running out of food before we found new sources of food, have left many emaciated and sick. Katherine was actually one of the more vibrant among us. I believe she died more of grief and shock than other maladies.

There is more news, but none of more urgency than informing you about the fate of your sister. I trust Governor Bradford's letter will contain all the other news such as the list of those departed from us, the babies born, the exciting meeting with the Indians.

There has been good among our challenges. The day the Indian king called on our community was thrilling. Oh, how I wish you could have seen it! The colors and beads and feathers they wear are lovely.

I long for the day when we will be together again so I can tell you more about that.

For now though, it is both my burden and blessing to be the one selected to write you about Katherine. You may be proud of her, as I truly am. She carried herself well through every struggle and setback we encountered since that day last July when we left you standing on the dock watching us all pull away from you. It seems a lifetime ago. It is actually less than a year. When life is so full of upsets and surprises, the sense of time changes.

A day can feel like a month. A month can feel like only a portion of a day.

Kathryn Brewster Haueisen

I close with the assurance your sister lived boldly, loved generously, worked diligently, and consoled me greatly in my longing to spend time with you, dearest friend. May the Lord who brought us all together, now console you as you bear the force of this news.

Your friend,
Mary Brewster

~ ~ ~

William read the letter without comment. He folded it and sealed it and set it down on the table. Still without speaking, he pulled me close to his chest and embraced me in his arms. When he released me, I saw the tears that washed down his cheeks. Still without speaking, he picked up the letter and left to add it to the many other letters and documents Master Jones would soon carry back to London. From there some would be delivered to our investors to give an accounting of our dire situation. Others would eventually reach our families and friends in England and the Lowlands.

Watching William carry the letter away felt like somehow releasing Katherine's spirit to reunite it with her sister. I felt at peace, accepting there was nothing more I could do, and knowing I had done what I could to offer a bit of comfort to someone I loved very much.

Chapter 24

April 10, 1621

Writing a letter to Bridget about the death of her sister was the hardest thing I have done since we first arrived here. It makes me ache so much for her, and Patience and Fear, and the joyous fellowship we knew together in Leyden. My heart feels like cast iron in my chest tonight.

A couple of weeks later Master Jones announced he would pull up anchor and sail back to England as soon as the winds were favorable. He had grown close to us and left as many supplies as he could do without. We had our gardens planted, but so far there was little other than peas to eat beyond what the men hunted or the fish they caught. We were still malnourished, clinging to our hopes the crops would do well. Master Jones offered, "Hate to leave you in such pitiful straights. Guess I could find room for a few of you if'n any of you want to go back to England."

William shook his head vigorously before I could determine if I wanted to go back or not. The idea of spending one more minute on that bloody ship was enough to set my stomach quivering. But then, thinking about all the tasks to be done here, with far fewer of us to tend to them than when we first anchored, was also a troublesome thought. The idea of seeing Bridget again was a very strong pull. But in the end it didn't matter what I wanted. All the men agreed we would stay.

That was the end of that.

I resigned myself to my fate, grateful that at least I would not have to experience another long voyage. I had learned well that when there is nothing I can do about a situation, my best response is to do nothing; to focus on other matters. My joints ached more days than not. I was not confident I could survive another voyage. I was almost grateful for the swollen joints because they distracted me from regretting too much not being able to return to Europe.

Then a fear nibbled at me like a dog chewing a bone.

Might it be that in deciding to stay, there would soon be nothing left of us beyond our bones? Would some future group of colonists come to find our few modest homes abandoned? Well, what was done could not be undone. Master Jones and his sailors sailed away in mid-April and we stayed.

I stood with William and all the others on shore as the *Mayflower* grew smaller and smaller. I stared out at the horizon long after the ship disappeared from view all together. William finally pulled me away and, with his arm locked in mine, steered me back to our cottage. I didn't accomplish a single thing more that day. I sat as if in a trance, trying to absorb it all. Though I came to detest that bloody ship, it was my last connection to home and all that was familiar. I sat on a small stool in our earthen floored cottage, surrounded with work that never ended and problems that grew faster than the weeds in the garden.

The spinning wheel I managed to keep safe aboard the ship with the other cargo beckoned my attention. The wool I brought would not wind itself into skeins of yarn any more than the pieces of fabric tucked away in our trunk would sew themselves into britches for Love. Mercifully he outgrew them before they were too worn out, so I could

Kathryn Brewster Haueisen

pass them on the Wrestling. I would have to get to work soon, but for now, I sat while William read and the children occupied themselves outside snapping kindling and playing sword fights with the sticks.

After a while, my husband set his open book on his lap and looked over at me, as if he just realized I was in the room with him. "We have done it, Mary. We have done it! We are in our own home in our new plantation. The crops grow in our first garden, all in our family are alive and well, and we have a peace treaty established with the Indians. What a marvel to accomplish all this in less than a full year."

I tried to match his mood. I know I promised to go where he went and be obedient to him undo death. Many times in recent years I felt like perhaps I had already died, but my body just did not yet realize it. With the *Mayflower* gone, there was no hope I could return to my family and friends in Leyden or England. I realized I would never see either place again. I felt tears forming and pushed my fingernails into my palms to keep them from spilling over.

I don't think William recognized my discouragement, or more likely, he didn't know what to do about my melancholy mood. Whichever it was, he left to look for the children, leaving me to my thoughts. I simmered in distress until I was worn out from it.

I sat for a while with my eyes closed trying to remember details from our homes in Leyden and Scrooby and listening to the sounds around me. With the door open I could hear birds nearby and the faint sound of the waves in the bay not far away. Tired of being sad, I decided to go for a walk.

When I did, I was smacked with a good dose of reality.

Over toward the brook I spotted Mr. Winslow and Widow Susanna walking together. She had Peregrine in a basket strapped on her back. They stopped once they reached the water's edge. Mr. Winslow helped her set the basket on the ground and she then pulled Peregrine out of it. They stood side by side, gazing at the brook, I suppose astonished at how full it was with herring.

Watching them, my melancholy turned to shame.

Only a few weeks earlier Elizabeth Winslow dragged herself from her sick bed to join me and the children while her brave husband went to the Indians the day of the treaty. She was too weak to come out to watch the festivities, and likely also too worried about the fate of her husband. She perked up when he returned to our settlement unharmed. We all prayed she might be spared; but it was not meant to be. Even so, Mr. Winslow carried on through his grief to keep us going. And poor Susanna kept going after both her husband and his servant died, leaving her to provide for Resolved and little Peregrine on her own.

My troubles were but a pebble in my shoe compared to the ones these two God-fearing Christians endured with nary a harsh word to anyone. Seeing them carrying on as though they had not suffered afflictions made my skin hot with shame.

Rather than rebuke me for my foul mood, William tended the children, leaving me room to find my way. It is odd how seeing my neighbors enjoying the day at the brook changed my perspective. If these two, who had each known much greater trials than I had, could find serenity and hope, I should follow their example.

I went in search of William with a renewed sense of purpose and determination to make life for him and our household as pleasant as possible. I found him patiently letting the children tie bundles of sticks for kindling.

I loved him all over again for the kindness he showed me that day.

Watching him with our sons and the orphan lad made my angst evaporate and my heart swell with pride. I truly admired him for everything he did to help our little group make this journey. His faith never wavered. I wondered if I might someday acquire the same measure of trust and hope in the Lord's providence.

Following that heartwarming event at the brook, I watched a new love blossom. In May Mr. Winslow and Widow White announced their marriage and I felt pure delight. We all needed something to celebrate and break the routine. A wedding was just the thing.

Kathryn Brewster Haueisen

It was our first one and it happened on the 12th of May, 1621 as we approached our first summer. It was the first civil service Governor Bradford performed.

We each brought something to contribute to the fine celebration feast. For hours we laughed, sang and told outrageous stories from other weddings we remembered from far away and long ago. My spirits felt as light as the ripples of clouds drifting overhead. In preparation for the wedding, some men went hunting. They returned with a deer and several waterfowl. It was sheer joy.

That first wedding did much to confirm our resolve to make our little community thrive. Regardless of our troubles, we had one another and love always found a way. The differences between our Leyden fellowship and the Strangers sent by the investors faded day by day, melding us into a small, but determined new fellowship of pilgrims.

Governor Bradford crossed his arms and sighed with satisfaction at the sight of us celebrating together. "All great and honorable actions are accompanied with great difficulties, and both must be enterprised and overcome with answerable courage."

We had overcome with good courage, now we were one new community of planters far away from what was familiar, working as one body to establish our new home.

Chapter 25

April 12, 1621

The ship is gone a week now, and with it my last connection to home. I gave Master Jones letters for Jonathan, Patience, Fear and Bridget. He will go back to England. Who knows if he will truly care about any of us enough to see that the correspondence gets to Leyden? And even if they should, by the grace of God, reach their intended recipients, how long will it be before we ever see another ship that might carry a response?

Though this cottage is packed with children and visitors each day, I feel totally alone without my daughters and Bridget. I must go on. It appears to suit the good Lord's pleasure that I live. For the sake of others in our fellowship, I must go on.

With the *Mayflower* gone and the glow of the wedding celebration dimming, we settled into our first summer. The few hens and roosters we'd brought with us blessed us with both eggs and chicks, which delighted the children. They carried the newly hatched chicks around like the precious treasures they were. We built pens to try to contain the pigs, but soon gave up the idea of keeping them contained. We set them free outside the palisade to roam and forage for themselves, away from our gardens. We set up three-sided shelters for them along the outside of the palisade and gave them treats under their shelters in order to have them think of those spaces are their home, it kept them safer and healthier in storms and easier to shoot a boar if one was needed. The dogs not only helped find them, but also led us to one of the pigs when we needed one to butcher.

By fall we had ample food to last us through the second winter and all of us were looking much healthier with fresh food added to our menus. Governor Bradford declared we should suspend work for three days and refresh our spirits as we rested our bodies. That was news as good as the cries of "Land, Ho!" heard not quite a year earlier. The men decided to parade all around the village, firing their muskets as they went, to announce the official holiday from labor. As they approached the gate leading out into the forest to hunt for game for the holiday of rest, they were greeted by several dozen Indians all whooping and hollering and dashing in through the gate!

Having had only pleasant exchanges with them before, we were shocked at the sight. Captain Standish called out for all the men to line up with their muskets at the ready. Governor Bradford marched to the Indians with his hands stretched out, showing he carried no weapon. Squanto sprinted from where he had been sampling food from one of the tables set up with some of the bounty from our harvest.

He called out to the Indians in their language. Then, with a grin that went across the whole bottom half of his face, he explained, "They heard you shoot. They thought you were being attacked. Then they saw the gate open and thought you needed help. Thus, they approached prepared to defend you."

Governor Bradford's jaw dropped. "They came to defend us?"

"Yes. Because of the talk you made with them."

Kathryn Brewster Haueisen

"Right!" remembered Governor Bradford. "Tell them, we celebrate. We have food." He waved his arm around the village where many families had pulled their tables from their homes out to set up a community feast. "We have plenty and we are giving thanks to our great God for the abundance. And tell them how honored we are that they rushed to help us."

Squanto translated. The Indians spoke among themselves. Squanto turned back to Governor Bradford. "We will celebrate with you. We will go and say the English are not in trouble. The English are happy. We will come back and be happy with you."

They were true to their word and returned a few hours later, all in all over ninety of them, along with several venison, turkeys and other things to add to our table. Some of their women came with them and I longed to speak to them. But since no one bothered to translate for us, we had to settle for staring and smiling at one another between chores to coordinate the massive amounts of food required to feed so many.

There were only four of us adult women still alive to manage all the food preparation. The children helped, but at times it was as much work to supervise them as it was to do without their assistance.

The Indian women helped too, of course. However, not understanding one another's language, we could not truly help one another.

Chapter 26

November 15, 1621

I cannot believe it has been months since I made an entry. The summer kept us very busy. We worked at one task or another from early morning until nine o'clock since we had good light by which to work. Then the wonderful fall harvest. How good it was to fill our stomachs with all manner of fine food and try to make conversation with our Indian neighbors. Those were a wondrous few days.

We approach a year now since arriving and are in so much better state of affairs than at that time.

My joy increased a hundred-fold after the harvest celebration. It was toward the end of November, about a year after we first saw land, and the leaves were now off the trees again. This time we were prepared for winter with plenty of food and wood already stocked and stacked. With no garden to tend to, most of us women turned to creating things inside and mending other things that had worn out or broken to get them ready for spring. The early winter days fell into an easy routine.

The children saw it first.

Then a few men collecting lobsters.

A ship! A ship on the horizon!

The boys shouted, "Look! It sails toward us!"

Seeing a ship flying a British flag thrilled me. My heart stopped for a minute, then began beating faster and faster. I pulled up my skirts and ran as fast as my old legs could carry me down to the edge of the water to see it for myself. Love, Wrestling and Richard joined me, jumping up and down with glee. William sauntered over and waited with us as we watched the crew do their work. It seemed as though they took hours to drop the anchor, pull down the sails, latch them to the masts, and lower their long boat over the edge.

I saw Jonathan! Dear Lord! I saw my son! Setting aside all dignity, I called out, "Jonathan! Jonathan! Here, look here! Do you see us?"

When he saw us, he waved back, swinging his arms back and forth in wide gestures. He started to rise from his seat in the longboat, but nearly lost his balance, so he sat back down. He gripped the boat side with one hand and kept waving furiously with the other. When the longboat was close to shore, he sprang over the side and trudged through knee-high water toward us. As anxious as I was to embrace him, I had to compete with Love and Wrestling, who were equally excited and more adept at negotiating the uneven rocky beach. They hopped up and down like frogs, and would have run into the water if William had not grabbed hold of their collars and forbid them do so. The instant their older brother had one foot on dry ground they lunged toward him, latching on faster than fleas hop on a dog. Jonathan swung them both around and then set them down.

When it was my turn, he hugged me so hard I thought he might crush me, but I did not mind one mite. To gaze into his face after sixteen long months made me the happiest I had been since before William's arrest. Looking at him that day felt like looking at William when we were young and full of naïve assumptions about how our lives

Kathryn Brewster Haueisen

would unfold. Jonathan with his long, narrow face, blue eyes and tiny grin was like seeing William again in his youth.

Then it was William's turn. William generally kept his emotions carefully guarded, rarely expressing more than a few words of affection or offering a quick hug and peck on my cheek if others could witness us together. But that day even unflappable William reached first to shake our son's hand and then pulled him in for a long embrace. I do believe I saw a few tears on his wrinkled cheeks.

Jonathan brought me letters from Patience, Fear and Bridget Robinson. The letters were dearer to me than anything else the ship delivered. I was sad I could not also embrace my daughters, but at least their letters assured me they were well. Jonathan told me they had not found suitable young men in our absence. I surprised myself to realize that news didn't make me sad, but rather relieved. Patience was already twenty-one and Fear not far behind her. It was time they married, but I clung to the hope they would not marry until they joined us here. Though likely candidates were sorely missing on this side of the ocean. I thought perhaps potential husbands came with Jonathan on this ship now bobbing out where the *Mayflower* had been for so many months. I wondered why William couldn't arrange husbands for our daughters. If it troubled him, he didn't speak of it.

As things went, there actually were several suitable mates on the *Fortune,* but that was of no use when our daughters remained in Holland. I thanked the good Lord that Jonathan had arrived and prayed that Patience and Fear would come on the next ship. Perhaps these single men would have cottages built and waiting for brides by the time the next ship arrived. I looked over the other young men and wondered if any of them might one day be a son-in-law.

Soon they were unloading the precious few supplies they carried in the cargo. They brought barely enough to feed themselves, obviously unaware of how precarious our situation had been, and still was with these new young men to feed. The treasure of the whole ship was a champion milking nanny goat whose babies would be in great demand once she had her first set of twins. She was a lovely creature, and her sweet temperament and large amounts of milk kept us from turning our disappointment on her; the disappointment that we had been hoping for a few cows to make it over on the next Separatist ship. Alas, cows were going to be still a few years off in our future.

Jonathan proved himself an asset straight away, helping build more houses to accommodate the *Fortune* passengers. He also showed a knack for trading, acquiring many useful things from our Indian neighbors. As a small lad he often found treasures—a peculiarly shaped stone or the bones of some long-since deceased bird. He'd bring these home and offer to trade them for some treat or toy. He could always talk younger children into giving him what he wanted by convincing them they needed whatever oddity he found. He inherited his father's smooth tongue.

The *Fortune* brought high hopes for desperately needed supplies and additional help, but those hopes were soon shaken. Between the pitiful lack of supplies and the news and letters it brought us; our hopes soon turned as sour as the goat milk that would have to make do. Our harvest and long celebration did much good for morale, but our challenges were unrelenting. We had sufficient food stored to feed our small fellowship through this second winter; however, we were not prepared to feed so many young, hungry young men as now joined us. Their own food larder was all but diminished after their voyage.

We had food again, but we needed things we could not yet provide for ourselves. With no cows, we had no butter. At least the *Fortune* brought a few goats in addition to the prized nanny, so we could have goats' milk to make cheese. It was a sorry substitute for the rich cheeses we savored before, but an improvement of our situation. We needed tools, fabric to replace clothes worn to a state of rags, and beer, until our hops matured enough to make our own. And more workers if we were truly to turn a profit for the investors. The *Fortune* did bring more laborers, but it was a matter of hours before we understood the great divide between our hopes and their expectations.

In addition to more mouths to feed, the *Fortune* also brought news of the world we left behind. Some of this news we could have

Kathryn Brewster Haueisen

done without, as it was quite stressful. Our friend Deacon Robert Cushman presented Governor Bradford a letter from a head Adventurer, Thomas Weston, that greatly shocked and discouraged us. It was addressed to our departed Governor Carver and offered not even a crumb of Christian charity regarding our desperate situation.

Deacon Cushman entrusted the nasty letter to Governor Bradford, who read it at the next Sabbath meeting, with red cheeks in a tight, high-pitched voice. He read sentiments such as, "that you sent no lading back with this ship is strange, and very properly resented. I know your weakness was the cause of it; and I believe more weakness of judgment than weakness of hands . . . give us account, as particularly as you can, how our money was laid out . . . And consider that the life of this business depends on the lading of our ships. If you provide a satisfactory amount, so that I may recoup the great sums I disbursed for the former voyage, and must do for this one, I promise you I will never forsake this enterprise, though all the other Adventurers should do so."

When he finished, Mr. Bradford folded the letter, his hands shaking, and said, "This, this wretched man apparently could not muster a feather's worth of compassion for us! He thinks only about increasing his already full coffers." He turned to look at the young men who arrived along with shocking letter.

"I thank the Lord Almighty that we have you here to help us. As you will soon learn, the amount of work required of us is a good deal greater than the number well enough to do it. Yet, I am sorely disappointed that Mr. Weston has sent no additional provisions or other items to assist us in meeting his demand for additional lading."

The men discussed how to respond to Mr. Weston's greed. I left with the other women to prepare a meal for everyone, a daunting task since we now numbered over seventy hungry people. The condition of the new arrivals was hardly better than ours had been a year earlier. We started by setting them up with bedding on the floor of the Common House to ensure all the sick were in one place to nurse them more easily. The few healthy ones were assigned to various cottages and would be the first to move into new ones we would build. Time to crowd together once again.

Further challenging us, most of the *Fortune* passengers were young, single men with wild ideas. They expected to carry on as though they owed no account to anyone for what they did. Some helped, but many challenged our routines more than assisted. We knew we had to labor without ceasing to fill the hold of the ship before it sailed back, or risk Mr. Weston abandoning us with no further assistance. We had only a few weeks to do so because the ship was set to sail to England soon.

We worked tirelessly to procure wood, beaver furs, cod, sassafras, salted game meat and other commodities to send back with the *Fortune*. Filling the ship, when we needed to be laying up provisions for our second winter. That is, most of us worked. Convincing some of the young men to do their share proved work in itself. Whether they worked or found ways to avoid it, they ate and consumed enormous quantities of precious food.

My husband preached to encourage the younger men to accept they were now part of a community and must do their share. This was a plantation, which meant it was not just a town; Plimoth Plantation was created to be a collection of homes and families that worked together to provide for themselves. This meant all were a part of the work so that all could be part of the harvest.

While William worked on their minds, I was eagerly looking ahead to the day I might again see Bridget and my daughters.

I decided to write Bridget another letter, as well as the one I composed for my daughters. I wrote my letters by light from a candle and the fire at the end of each day. Writing them gladdened my heart. I could clearly see Bridget in my mind, holding my letter, as she sat at the table where we had often worked together.

Kathryn Brewster Haueisen

November 29, 1621

My dearest Bridget,

*As I write you our men and the **Fortune's** crew load what few provisions our impoverished colony can send back to the merchant Adventurers. It shall be far less than they demand, but this partial payment for our debt will perhaps convince them we do honor our obligations. Jonathan was one of the first off the ship and I wish you could have seen our reunion. Love and Wrestling were ecstatic when they saw him. It was a moment of sheer joy. Even the More child who never knew Jonathan got caught up in the excitement.*

William has prepared his own letter for Pastor Robinson to share with the fellowship. As you must know from a previous letter I sent, William Bradford now assumes the duties of governor and serves us faithfully. He works from very early morning until dark on our behalf. He is a good man. You would marvel at how he has matured into a level-headed, fair and compassionate leader who knows when to chastise and when to praise.

Bridget, I count on you to receive what I feel I must tell someone but cannot bring myself to confess to anyone here. My heart has been broken often since you and I last saw each other. I write this letter for you alone and beg you not share it with others. I would not want any to think me less than a loyal helpmate to William. He and the other men remain so confident we have faithfully followed the Lord's injunction to go forth into all the world, making new disciples. I confess to you, and to you alone, that I wonder if that is truly the case.

Their efforts to convert the Indians are futile. The Indians cause us little trouble; indeed, they have helped us enormously, but show little interest in learning more about the faith that compelled our men to set forth on this perilous path. William is a dear man and I am grateful for him, truly I am. But dear friend, I am so alone here. The companionship of two of the London women, Elizabeth Hopkins and Elinor Billington is some comfort. I believe you would come to treasure them as I have. Your sister Katherine was always a good friend to me and I miss her, as I know you must as well.

I am worn out from tending to the orphans and bereaved. I am the oldest woman here and they all turn to me in times of uncertainty. Staying strong to keep them all calm has worn me out. It is a little better now, but the younger women still look to me for comfort that I struggle to provide. At last Jonathan is with us again and that has helped greatly!

He tells me Patience and Fear fare well enough. I thank you for your tender mercies toward them. I am so grateful they have you. I look out across the bay with anticipation that any day I might see another mast and billowing sails approaching, bringing them – and you – to us.

The Indian who speaks English often visits. He shows us better ways to manage in this strange place. I finally met a few Indian women at our fall festival, but with no one bothering to translate for us, the best we could do was share some of the food and laugh together at the antics of the children and baby animals. I hope eventually I might get to know more about their lives, which are so different than my own. One Indian mother let me hold her infant daughter I looked into her black

Kathryn Brewster Haueisen

eyes and chubby cheeks and cooed at her like I did my own babies. I was rewarded with a big smile. She stuck her little tongue out and made smacking sounds that melted my heart. I find myself smiling now as I write you about it. What a wondrous thing it is to hold a baby. That is a bond that connected us even though we spoke barely a word of one another's language.

This has been quite the adventure, so different from our former days together. Please do not share this letter with the others; but do pass along the news that after a grim start, we are settling in. We are grateful for the new people who have joined us and eager for the rest of the fellowship to join us here.

Your dearest friend,

Mary Brewster

Chapter 27

November 20, 1621

Having Jonathan at the table again makes everything seem better. The winter chill is less cold. The food tastes better. He knows how to get a laugh from the boys and the sound of their giggling and laughing lightens the mood for all of us. I think William also truly appreciates having Jonathan's company.

Things are much better now. I wish the other young men would work as hard as Jonathan. I suppose over time, with my husband's words and Governor Bradford's prodding, they will.

Deacon Cushman preached the last Sabbath before the *Fortune* sailed. He looked at the newly arrived young men, looking into each man's face without speaking. Then he pulled himself up as tall as he could and, using a strong, deep voice, addressed them. "Young men, I observe that you desire to sever all ties to those who made your voyage possible. I fear your youthful passion may be stronger than your sense of reality and necessity. Loathsome though you may find those who control the funds that sustain you, you must set aside your childish desires to do as you please. You see wherever you look here the progress these who arrived before have made, without so much as an hour of your labor. This they did in the midst of sorrows you cannot fathom.

"I implore you to set your minds to imagining how much greater this plantation in the wilderness will be when you commit yourselves to helping in all manner possible. It is only by the grace of God and the Lord's looking over us that we have come this far. This plantation is of and for our fellowship. We shall go forward only with the further guidance and instruction of the Lord. Elder Brewster guides us and teaches us the Lord's ways. Governor Bradford leads us faithfully and more than adequately. It is your part to listen to them and obey their instructions.

"Think first of the welfare of those who welcome you, who share the fruits of their labor and the very homes they built. Think on those things and do not yield to your lust for freedom from responsibilities. This shall be for your own benefit as well as the others gathered here this morning. Apply your vigor to those pursuits that further establish this plantation. Bend your will to that of your elders, for this is the will of God and the way to peace and harmony. If you do not, you may anticipate arrest warrants will follow and you will be forever running alone until you are caught and hanged."

I credit Deacon Cushman for trying. Though valiant, his efforts failed to persuade most of the young men to harness their youthful passion away from pursuing their own interests. We had to discuss turning them out of our colony for two major reasons; we could not feed any who would not contribute to gathering game and supplies and we could also be arrested for harboring fugitives once the arrest warrants finally reached us. They had only until the next ship arrived to change their lazy ways.

The *Fortune* sailed on the 21st of December and was barely out of sight when the full measure of their rebellious ways surfaced. Though it was a Sabbath, we set out to work the balance of the day, as was our custom while we were still building homes. Some among the new

Kathryn Brewster Haueisen

arrivals refused to work, telling Governor Bradford it was against their consciences to work on the Sabbath. Since most of the newcomers were not from our covenant fellowship in Leyden, he allowed for it.

But when he returned to the village from hunting, he found them out in the streets playing all manner of games. He took their games and sporting things away, insisting, "If they make keeping of the day a matter of devotion, let them remain in their houses; but there should be no gaming in the streets."

We were well used to the escapades of the Billington boys but were not prepared to have to discipline adult men! It was a consternation that nearly did me in. William urged me to apply patience and gentle persuasion. I was more inclined to apply a long wooden paddle.

Annoying and dangerous as some of the Billington boys' stunts had been, I could overlook them as the reckless adventures common among young boys. Indeed, once the danger of their impulsive behavior was resolved, I found their behavior humorous. Though of course I was careful not to let them catch me smiling at the ingenuity of their feats.

We never knew what fool thing one or the other of the Billington boys would try next. Their escapades were legendary. People still talked about the day aboard the *Mayflower* when young Francis Billington took his father's fowling piece and fired it, only a few feet away from an open barrel of gunpowder. After a thorough cussing out from the crew, he slunk back to his family. When Master Jones heard about it, he slammed his fist on his table and reached for a bottle of whiskey.

Then there was John Junior Billington's great adventure.

Shortly after we anchored in the bay, he wandered off alone and got lost in the woods for five days. He claimed an Indian led him back to the clearing where our men were at work, though no one ever saw any Indian that day or any other for many more months.

William was quick to point out that the Lord used the boy's disobedience to assist us. John Junior climbed high up in a tree to look for his father and he spotted a small inland lake, which proved to be a most beneficial source of water. Poor Elinor did her best to keep up with her sons, but Lord Almighty, what a job that was. Keeping an eye on them became a community effort, one we accepted as part and parcel of learning how to come together in our new settlement.

The Billington boys were mischievous, yet they were also loving and full of energy when chopping wood and doing other chores; they would probably turn out to be great hunters and protectors for our next generation of Separatists.

The young men brought by the *Fortune* could have been a true blessing, if only they had decided to help.

I was proud of Jonathan who eagerly pitched in to do whatever task Governor Bradford assigned. Though the governor was only a couple of years older than he, Jonathan expressed no resentment about doing his bidding.

Kathryn Brewster Haueisen

Chapter 28

September 6, 1622

Today marks two years since we left England.
We have certainly accomplished a great deal in these
two years. Week by week our little village grows larger.
We now record more births than deaths—that even
includes the animals; blessing us with abundance. There
is nothing like the birth of a baby to elevate one's mood.

Governor Bradford is continuing to be a fine
leader. He and his assistants bring order and calm
allowing most of our days to pass in tending to our
chores in peace and harmony, though of course, never
completely free of challenges.

As our second spring approached, the men decided each family should finally have their own garden. Each new cottage had a lot extending back fifty feet, the width determined by the size of each family. Our cottage was as full as any of them, so our lot was about fifty feet across.

While I made furrows in the soil, I set the children to work pulling out stones to place in a pile to be used to make a low fence around the garden.

The first plan that we share all things in common sounded better than it worked out. William believed the Adventurers considered it a good plan when they dictated that we should work together as one large family. The single men protested laboring for families, while families complained they worked hard enough to provide for themselves without also toiling for young men who could well do their own work. This quickly became a constant source of irritation. While we would still have to share the milk and cheese from the goats, the backbreaking gardening work would now be up to each family or person to stock their own larder.

William concluded at an evening meeting, "Each man's family may tend to their own garden, but we must continue to honor the covenant we forged back in Scrooby, when we broke away from the Established Church. We are here, laboring in a strange land under a hot sun for a singular purpose. Our purpose is to faithfully worship and obey our Lord. The Adventurers are far away in England, likely counting and recounting their money."

I chuckled to myself as I worked the furrows. William had such a way of putting things in perspective. He told Governor Bradford, "I have a suggestion to send to them. Come on the next ship and observe for themselves how our community works."

Governor Bradford laughed out loud. "Aye, yet I think it best we pray the good Lord watch over them in England where they belong. I've challenges enough without the merchant investors coming to pester us in person."

"Again, you demonstrate your wisdom, my young friend," laughed William.

~ ~ ~

Kathryn Brewster Haueisen

By the first fall harvest celebration there had been many visits between our men and the Indian King Massasoit. When the *Fortune* people came, we had to dissuade them from doing anything that might offend the Indians and stir up trouble. Governor Bradford and Mr. Winslow, along with William and others, had many stern talks with some of the young men who had not lived through all we had. Nor had they seen the day of the treaty and all the resulting visits back and forth. These new folks had the luck to quickly recover from malnutrition after the ocean voyage by eating our food, not the months of terror and wondering if we would all die on a cold winter night. We had not only respect for the Indians, but also knew our mutual aid agreement was crucial for sustaining a peaceful future.

We saw our Indian neighbors occasionally, especially Squanto. He seemed more at home among us than among his own people. We were grateful for his help, though I wondered why he didn't care to spend more time with his own kind. After a while Squanto decided he preferred to live in our village. I thought that was perhaps because it had been his home before Shipmaster Hunt kidnapped him and the others. I felt for the lad. He was about the age of Jonathan but had no living family. Apparently, our ways did not bother him.

As we got to know him better, he told us of the travesties he suffered. Kidnapped. Hauled away in the hold of a ship. Rescued and taken in by an English merchant. Then excited to find a way home, only to find his village destroyed and abandoned. All gone. My heart ached for him. I even felt myself wanting to reach out to embrace him, but caught myself in time.

That wasn't appropriate for a married woman.

A proper English woman simply did not go about touching people who were not of her own family, and even at that, such a bold show of affection was best reserved for special moments. But I did have sympathy for his plight. And I was grateful for his willingness to teach me and others how to cajole the most from the land. We needed every blade, kernel, and pod we could grow. Squanto often walked among us pointing to where things had been for his Patuxet people. That left me with the strangest combination of grief and gratitude: grief for him, gratitude that the good Lord led us to this place with our own guide to teach us the ways of this vibrant young land.

"Be cautious, dear Mary," William warned when I expressed my sympathy for Squanto. "It appears the Massasoit does not fully trust Squanto because he speaks English, it renders him and his council dependent on Squanto to explain things. Mr. Winslow told me their Massasoit wonders if Squanto always interprets truthfully or if he twists things to his advantage. We are as dependent on him as the Massasoit is. Though he has helped us greatly, it does seem peculiar that he is so eager to ingratiate himself to us, while reluctant to resume closer relations with his own kind. You have been sheltered from some of the ugliness of those who connive and deceive to achieve their own personal plans. So, I warn you, do not be unduly persuaded by his tales."

As William spoke, I felt the burn of humiliation spreading throughout my body. All my life I had been taught to have compassion for the plight of others. Now my husband was telling me perhaps that compassion was a weakness and not a desired quality after all, at least not in all situations. I didn't know quite what to think. At that moment I felt a wave of dread wash over me and wished with an immensity that frightened me that I could turn time back and be back in England before I ever said "I will" to William.

How much simpler my life was before I accepted William's proposal and followed him on this quest to shed all the excessive demands of the modern church. I said nothing but returned to shelling dried peas to store for the winter.

Overall, life had settled into a hard, but productive situation.

We had our covenant agreement by which we governed ourselves and our investors; we had an agreement with the Indians. But now some among the new arrivals seemed determined to act according to their own will. Conflicts erupted from time to time, but the compact drawn up while still on the ship helped sustain us through such times and kept a basic peace between Saints and Sinners.

Kathryn Brewster Haueisen

Any signs of bickering or rebellion were a significant threat to us, and could not be tolerated.

We were well aware that our situation was still precarious. It was a constant topic at our community meetings about some of us not understanding the importance of working together.

~ ~ ~

The Indian king proved himself a faithful leader and an equally good neighbor. Our men soon came to highly regard him.

At the start there were some misunderstandings between our communities. Governor Bradford, Mr. Winslow, Mr. Hopkins and William called on him shortly after the day of the March Treaty. They sought to secure use of some property to graze our few animals, goats always being hungry. When the men approached the Indian king to purchase land, he did not understand.

"What is this you call property? It cannot be the earth, for the land is our mother, nourishing all her children, beasts, birds, fish and all men. The woods, the streams, the fields, all belong to everybody to use to sustain life. How can one man say it belongs only to him?"

William told me no matter how hard they tried to explain about exchanging money for land, he did not comprehend what they wanted to do. "And even more baffling, he told the men they must talk to the woman. They manage the land."

I could not imagine that. I had heard of a few women who inherited land from their fathers or husbands if they had no brothers, but if they married, the land then belonged to their husbands to manage. That was the proper way of things.

Pastors preached often about the natural order of things, about how God ordered communities.

God provides for each man. The man provides for his wife and children. The wife takes care of the children until they are old enough to contribute their labor to the family.

That the Indians did not follow this pattern was astounding to me.

~ ~ ~

Since our men could not explain these concepts to the Indian king, we used what land we needed to provide for our growing colony without a contract. The Indians got upset when we let our pigs roam freely in land they indicated no one could own. Our men used the situation to again explain our ways, but they still did not seem to grasp the concept. In Europe all the land is owned by someone, mostly either the royalty or the bishops and archbishops of the church. The rest of the people worked the land, in exchange for their protection, always owing part of the harvest. We did not always like the system, but it had been in place farther back than anyone could remember, and it did seem a reasonable way to structure society. Everyone knew where they fit in and what was expected.

I shall always be grateful for the years we managed the manor and surrounding lands for Bishop Sandys in Scrooby.

I just shook my head when William explained the results of trying to negotiate land deals with the Indians. Confusion about this was a regular source of bewilderment and the topic of many conversations in our regular community meetings.

~ ~ ~

We approached our second harvest in far superior circumstances than our first, yet still needing to be cautious in how we managed our food and our affairs. And while our relations with our Indian neighbors

Kathryn Brewster Haueisen

seemed good, I could never quite let go of concerns that it could change or other tribes would come bringing war instead of trade. Our Indian friends seemed particularly agitated about the pigs in the woods, even when we offered them some of the meat.

One day in October, after our second harvest celebration, I was at work separating peas from dried pods to use as seeds for spring planting and thinking about what William told me about his many conversations with the Indians. Squanto assisted us in many ways, but it did seem as though he had some scheme in mind more often than not. I watched him closely as he and a few other Indians celebrated our second harvest with us. It was a much more subdued occasion than the first joyous three-day celebration, and fewer Indians joined us. I watched Squanto from the corner of my eyes and saw that he spent most of his time near Governor Bradford and Mr. Winslow. I wondered if he perhaps gathered information that he thought might benefit the Indian leader and put us to some disadvantage.

William, who had actually become rather good friends with the Indian king and was learning some of the language, said the king was just as suspicious of Squanto for the opposite reasons. "He seems to worry that what he tells me is not the whole truth, but rather the truth twisted to ingratiate himself to us while trying to make himself indispensable to both sides. Of course, we can speak directly now more readily than we could at the start. I think that may make Squanto feel a bit desperate to preserve his position as primary translator between us.

The thought made me heavy with worry as I played the memories in my mind. I set down my peas and stepped outside where I could see the hill behind our settlement. Looking up at it usually helped calm my thoughts. I silently recited the first lines from Psalm 121 that William taught me to love as much as he did. My favorite psalm brought me encouragement just as did a beautiful gray and white gull circling overhead, calling out while gliding peacefully overhead. "I will lift up mine eyes unto the mountains, from whence my help shall come. Mine help cometh from the Lord, which hath made the heaven and earth."

The thought of the psalm and the sight of the gull made me feel more settled in my situation. I returned to the cottage to resume my work.

~ ~ ~

In November Governor Bradford and several others took Squanto with them in our shallop to visit one of the Indian villages. They were gone a week, busy doing some trading. They came back without Squanto. Governor Bradford explained, "After we visited the Indian village, Squanto grew terribly sick with some sort of fever. He started bleeding from his nose and became very weak. We pulled into a beach and he died in the shallop shortly after that. We buried him there. He fell ill and died within days. It was all such a shock."

Deacon Fuller asked for more details and when Governor Bradford supplied them, said, "That is suspicious. He has been exposed to all manner of illnesses from both his people and our own. He is young and healthy, and yet he suddenly catches a fever and dies in a matter of a couple of days after you visit one of the Indian villages? I wonder if their Indian king has had enough of him. Those symptoms seem like they are from poison."

The thought of it jolted me. Would these Indians be so savage as to poison one of their own?

I felt sympathy for this departed soul and anger and fear that our kingdom on earth was filled with thieves and murderers. But I was also grateful that my husband shielded me from so much of the evil around us.

~ ~ ~

Kathryn Brewster Haueisen

As the months unfolded, our lives slowly came to more closely resemble our former days in Leyden. When the first snow fell the second winter, I more readily cherished the beauty of the snowflakes as they fluttered gently down upon my cape. Knowing I could retreat to the warmth of a fire inside our cottage, I paused to survey the scene. The snow brightened the appearance of our little village. The beauty of it took my breath away. True, the cold weather made daily chores much more challenging, but compared to life on the ship, this hardly seemed a hardship at all.

Earlier in the fall the children treasured the freedom to scour the edge of the woods for sassafras. They tried to hunt squirrels and rabbits with their sling shots, though rarely succeeded. Whenever a boy did bring down a small animal, he strutted about as proud as any general coming home from a battle. They giggled with glee when the first snow fell and they were free to run about in it, making their snowballs and tracks and planning out how to make forts when the snow got deeper. Such simple pleasures created pleasant memories as we were building our new community.

As I got older, I grew to appreciate chores I could do while standing or sitting, rather than stooping as I had to do in the garden, milking short goats or while collecting eggs. My aging joints often complained long and loud if I did much bending or crouching near the ground.

One day William found me plopped down on the ground next to the garden, trowel in hand. My expression must have concerned him. "Are you well, Mary?"

"I am, but I find that I am in need of assistance to stand up." Without speaking, he reached down to take my hands and pull me up. "I shall instruct Love and Wrestling they must stay nearby when you work in the garden." And that was that. I was not released from the work, but it was some comfort to know I would not be abandoned outside in the elements if I could not rise again without assistance.

Preparing meals was a constant chore. At least I had the luxury of my fireplace and children to send to fetch water from the brook. We still made do often with dried meats, fish, fruits, and crunchy hard tack, but more and more we could also rely on the chickens for eggs. Lobsters were abundant. The sea was a wondrous source of food, but we lacked the tools needed do serious fishing without the *Speedwell*. Abandoning it meant also abandoning our hopes of using it to establish the fishing business we'd planned that would have soon paid our investors off and allowed us to thrive. That first plan quite literally did not hold water. Other ideas evolved about how we could repay our debt. Yet it was difficult with the minimum of tools at our disposal.

One of the few helpful pieces of cargo the *Fortune* brought included a clay oven. It was a traditional small, portable clay oven, like many others I once saw in England and Holland. I had never used one. We laughed as we learned. Our first few loaves went to the goats. Even they preferred to kick them about the field rather than try to eat them. With practice, our efforts soon improved.

With this oven and the flour inventory resupplied until we could grind oats next summer, we could return bread to our diets. We placed the oven on a table in the corner of the yard of the Common House, both to preserve our backs as we worked with it and to keep the heat and fire danger away from our precious meeting house. Baking bread soon became a social event for us women. It took all day to make a few large loaves and the men easily consumed a pound or more of bread every day. It was always the day before Sabbath when we set aside the time for making bread. Because we let the children add kindling all day, they loved bread day and were very proud of keeping the fire going at just the right level. We also sent the children running to the brook to fetch water to moisten the dough. It was a joke amongst the women on how much we like bread day because the children were always tired by evening and those were our most peaceful times.

Occasionally we mixed in rice, lentils, chestnuts or acorns, after someone roasted them a bit then ground them into powder. This added a bit of flavor and increased our production of bread for the day.

With no church bells ringing every quarter hour, I learned to read the height of the sun in the sky to tell time and actually got pretty

Kathryn Brewster Haueisen

good at gauging the time that way. The bread came out nicely browned once we mastered the proper length of time for rising and then additional time to bake the loaves. I knew a loaf was ready when I heard a hollow sound as I tapped a nice hard crust.

We placed the baked loaves in baskets and took them straight away to someone's cottage to cool. We learned quickly that letting them cool on a table outside only gave the goats a grand time tearing all our hard work to bits in minutes.

That was baking day. We started off baking only the day before Sabbath, planning to bake several times a week once we had an adequate supply of flour and fields growing more grain to replenish our supply. Between tending the garden, cleaning the fish, washing our clothes once or twice a month, mending things and cooking, I never lacked for something needing attention.

Overall, I was happy, or at least content again. My family was healthy. It was wonderful to have William and the boys, and I had the companionship of other women who were as sisters to me. But I ached to see my daughters again. I continued to pray they would soon join us. Meanwhile, our cottage provided good protection from the heat of the summer and the cold of the winter.

Chapter 29

July 25, 1623

Now I feel as though my life is complete. I have my daughters with me again! Any other troubles, small or large though they may be, pale in comparison to the relief I feel having them with me again. I sometime have to sit and rest to manage the soreness in my joints, but when I do, I know that Patience and Fear are close by and will come to me if I call out to them. That makes the pain bearable.

Life passed pleasantly, with only a few tense moments when conflicts erupted between different groups of Indians. We learned those living to the west of us were the Narragansetts and they were enemies of the Pokanokets who befriended us. I found it peculiar that the Indians had enemies among themselves. I struggled to tell one from another, but then I suppose perhaps they might have the same challenge among us. We spoke little of the Algonquin tongue, so we were limited as to what we could find out. After Squanto died, our limited knowledge of their language and ways left us at a great disadvantage.

Mr. Winslow proved to be our best protection from the tensions and the uncertainty about if and when we were expected to take our muskets and help the Pokanokets. Mr. Winslow made numerous visits to the great Indian king, sometimes going alone; other times taking William, Governor Bradford, Mr. Hopkins, Captain Standish or others. William always reported that their visits were very congenial and encouraging, so we continued to believe we were safe enough.

Nonetheless, Myles Standish thought it best that we be prepared. He worked diligently to keep our men trained and ready, having them march up and down with their muskets at regular intervals every week. I thought perhaps he was too quick to turn to his weapons to resolve problems, but it was reassuring to know he was prepared and always concerned about our security.

Governor Bradford was slowly turning the renegade young men from the *Fortune* into respectable enough gentlemen who did their portion of the work. They continued to chaff at the idea they had to be part of the community, but between the governor's discipline and warning about arrests and hangings, William cajoling and, I am proud to boast, Jonathan's example, they began to settle down.

By July of 1623 the settlement felt like my home.

~ ~ ~

I was enjoying a summer walk along the shore, taking pleasure in the breeze coming off the bay on a warm July afternoon when I thought I saw something on the horizon. Whales were always fun to watch. In hopes of seeing a big one I put my hands above my eyes to shield them from the sun and squinted to see better.

A ship!

Kathryn Brewster Haueisen

It was a ship coming! I called out to those who were closest to me to come confirm it. As we watched it cross the bay, I held my breath until I thought my lungs would burst. My heart beat faster as the approaching sails grew larger. Soon sweat was rolling down my face, but I didn't want to move to some shade and miss seeing who the ship brought to us.

The sails snapped in the wind, as did the British flag the ship flew. At last, she came close enough to drop anchor. The crew scrambled all over the ship like ants attacking unattended food. The first men to climb down the ladder into the longboat were the crew. They assisted others until the boat was full before rowing to shore.

We crowded together on the beach. I stood on my tiptoes to see over the shoulders of those in front of me. As soon as the first crewman stepped onto the beach, we surrounded him, all shouting questions all at once at that first man who jumped out and wading to us ahead of the others. The crew still were sitting on the outside of the longboat so we couldn't see who or what else was in there.

"Have you brought livestock?"

"What fabric do you bring us?"

"Are there women aboard?"

Governor Bradford nodded consent, and Captain Standish fired his musket into the air away from the crowd. When the startled crowd grew silent, the governor took control. "Greetings and warmest welcome! We are eager to learn who you bring and what supplies you deliver. Dear fellow, give us a full account as I push back our crowd of eager families."

This first round of the longboat was quickly emptied and headed back to the ship for more.

As soon as he said women were aboard, I maneuvered my way to where I had a clear view of the longboat rocking in the surf. My heart thumped so hard I could feel it pulsing against my breastbone. And there they were, at long last. I took off my bonnet and waved it back and forth to draw their attention. When they saw it, they both called out as the boat approached. "Mama! Mama! We are here. We are arrived!"

Patience stepped ashore first and right behind her came Fear. They each pulled up their skirts and splashed hand in hand to me. We clung to one another for a long embrace; one that had to make up for the years without opportunity to touch or hear or see one another. All around us others jostled in search of their own family come from afar. Love and Wrestling maneuvered their way between us, forcing me to release my daughters. Then the four of them hugged, talking over one another, their voices growing louder and louder in a chorus of jubilation as we moved further away along the beach to get out of the excited crowd. *The missing pieces of my heart are here. I will finally be at peace.*

Jonathan and William approached together. "At last, you have arrived, and looking fit enough," Jonathan teased. "We must compare our sailing experiences." How fully he resembled his father's calm, unflappable way of handling any situation.

"There shall be time enough for that," said William as he kissed first Patience, then Fear, on the cheek. "Welcome home, my daughters. Welcome home." His hands went to his face, I suppose to wipe away tears he didn't want us to see. He walked back toward the houses, leaving us jabbering away like magpies as we followed. I had so much I wanted to say and ask. My relief at having them standing right before me caused a large lump to lodge in my throat and I had my own tears to manage.

My feet were soaked from standing where the water washed ashore and I was starting to feel the full effect of being out in the sun. I still had my bonnet in my hand and my hair felt hot to the touch. As I worked to get my bonnet back in place, I suggested we all retreat to our home to continue the conversation. With all my children gathered around as a mother hen gathers her chicks, we sat at our table as a whole family again. My joy was complete. They were all healthy and we were together again.

Typical of William, his first inclination was to read us a passage from his Bible and thank the Lord for this happy reunion. "I have pictured this very scene in my mind for so many months. And now at

Kathryn Brewster Haueisen

long last I do not have to imagine it. I, above all other men, I am blessed, blessed beyond measure."

That night we talked until the candle burned down to its holder.

~ ~ ~

The next day, with all the new arrivals settled in with various families, we met in the Common House. Governor Bradford asked Mr. Winslow to give a short report of our progress since the *Fortune* sailed away in December. Then he moved behind us where I watched him pace back and forth. He pulled something out of his vest and moved his lips as if practicing a speech.

When he resumed his proper place in front of us, he appeared tense, nervous and downcast. He waved the papers he'd pulled from his vest high in the air. "I have here another letter from our investors. "Everything we sent back on the *Fortune* to reduce our debt has been lost. Every last lading taken by pirates. They demand a double portion be returned on the *Anne* to compensate for it. That is the essence of this letter Thomas Weston sent to us on the *Anne*."

"Outrageous!" shouted Mr. Winslow. "They expect us to provide fruit from a new tree not yet grown. Blame for this loss cannot be placed upon us! That is the nature of investing, is it not? We must not let this blacken our reputation."

The room filled with groans and angry, loud cuss words.

"We are chained in debt like a mad dog. How will we ever be free of this obligation?" demanded Deacon Fuller.

His ire was contagious. Anger displaced the joy of only hours before. Forgotten was the happiness of listening to my daughters tell the news about the Robinson family and others we missed from Leyden. *Hope and despair are woven together until it seems impossible to have one without the other.*

I set aside any thoughts about Thomas Weston and the Adventurers who put him up to tormenting us. There were now enough of us that, with a little additional help from the Indians, we would manage quite well even if they never sent another ship. Let them fume. I had my family all together again. We had food and shelter. Life was hard, but our efforts began to show results, giving us good reason to be glad. For me, it was enough to have Patience and Fear with me.

The *Little James* arrived before the end of the month carrying precious cargo and only a few more people in need of shelter. And, wonder of wonders, it was arranged that the *Little James* would stay with us.

At last, we could embark on serious fishing efforts.

What a joyous turn of events to have my whole family gathered again and this new resource at our disposal. On top of all this joy, *Little James* brought a letter from Bridget . . .

June 5, 1623

> *My dear friend and sister in Christ,*
>
> *It is the strangest situation to send these members of our fellowship to you and wonder what the settlement that will receive them may be like by now. I pray for you daily, that your lot there is not too overwhelming. I have put your last letter to me in a secure place, so your request to keep it private shall be respected. Already I grieve for the absence of Patience and Fear in our home; yet even as I do, I also smile thinking about what joy you will know when you see them again.*
>
> *Isn't it peculiar how we cannot grasp one situation without letting go of another? I want to be*

Kathryn Brewster Haueisen

with you, but the cost of foregoing all that we have here seems too dear a price to pay. How I long to talk with you to learn how you manage this reaching out and letting go. How can we ever truly know when it is time to hold steadfast to what is or when it is time to venture forth with no certainty about where we go?

John speaks often about being led by the Spirit, but I know he too sometimes wonders if it is truly the Holy Spirit that summons him or his own desires. How can we know? Well, we will have to ponder such things without benefit of conversation. I shall miss your daughters and thank you for entrusting their care to me. I pray you have a most joyous reunion and will think kindly of me as you welcome them back to your home.

Perhaps the Lord shall yet arrange for us to be together again as well. I will cling to that hope. I look forward to another letter from you, perhaps one that reports on a good life for you there in Plimoth.

With great affection,
Your friend Bridget Robinson

Chapter 30

August 16, 1623

Governor Bradford has endured more in his young life than most do in twice as many years. Apparently, his son John fares well enough in Amsterdam. The boy was young enough when we left that he may not even remember his parents. There would be mercy in that. Though I suspect that Governor Bradford would like to have John join us here eventually. Perhaps that shall come to pass in the Lord's good time.

The *Anne* and *Little James* brought to us most of the rest of our Leyden fellowship who cared to join our experiment in the wilderness. The two ships also brought more people the Adventurers decided to send us. Again, we were obliged to somehow incorporate them into our fellowship. We had always hoped Pastor Robinson and Bridget would join us, but they were not among those who disembarked from *Little James*.

As had been the case with the *Fortune,* quite a number of the new arrivals turned out to be single young men, more intent on making themselves rich than contributing to the work of our new settlement. Even so, with the addition of new arrivals, memories of our desperate first year were displaced with happier times. Moments of joy steadily increased. With our family complete again, my days passed in a pleasant blur of activities.

One of the *Anne* passengers in particular gladdened the heart of our brave and hard-working Governor Bradford. It is a rare kind of hope and courage to commit oneself to love again after the kind of tragic grief he knew when Dorothy died. He knew Alice from earlier days in the Lowlands. Perhaps wanting to again know the happiness of sharing his life with a wife and having her keep a proper home for him, he proposed to Alice Carpenter by letter carried to her on the *Fortune.* She arrived on the *Anne.* They set their wedding for a few weeks later in August of 1623.

As a result of a number of mutually satisfactory visits between some of our men and Indian King Massasoit Ousa Mequin, the great leader accepted an invitation to attend the ceremony, bringing many of his men with him and looking as handsome as any gentleman who ever strolled the streets of London. He wore a bright red coat, a gift from Governor Bradford, along with a black wolfskin over his shoulder. He also brought one of his five wives to personally congratulate the governor.

Reminiscent of our first successful harvest in 1621, he again brought venison and a turkey to add to the happy day. Since it would not do for Governor Bradford to preside at his own wedding, that honor fell to his assistant, Isaac Allerton. The service was over practically before it began, and then we set to the festivities appropriate for our friend and leader who had so valiantly served us.

Laughter filled the air.

I wanted to speak with the Massasoit's wife to learn more about her life, but no one offered to translate for us. We were limited to observing one another, smiling and nodding our heads. After Squanto died, we all struggled to communicate. Through time and persistence we gradually increased our ability to speak with one another, but it was still very much a struggle for the women, as we had little occasion to meet together. At least the men grew in their ability to speak with each other. I rarely even saw Indian women, and when I did come upon one at the pond or in the woods, she was usually shy and scurried away as I approached.

William helped me learn a bit of their language, but when I tried to speak directly to one of the Indian women, her blank stares told me I didn't know enough to bridge the enormous language gap separating us. I doubt any Indian women knew English words. Generally, we sat in silence while the children played and the men discussed their hunting successes or trade business.

I had hoped the men would show a morsel of understanding about how much we women longed for feminine companionship, just as they treasured their manly fellowship. In spite of the lack of ability to speak to an Indian myself, it was thrilling to see so many gathered in their colorful attire.

Emmanuel Altham, sent by the Adventurers to compile a report on the status of our situation, also attended the wedding feast. He was so impressed, he wrote to his brother in England. "We feasted on venison and other such good cheer in such quantity that I could wish you some of our share." I fear it was a purposeful misstating of the situation, knowing it was a rare wedding celebration and not our daily fair.

Captain Standish capped off the afternoon by ordering the men to fire their many muskets both to celebrate and prove their preparedness to defend us, should the need arise. The Indians left their bows and arrows at the governor's home, and so responded by entertaining us with dancing. The *beat, beat, beat* of their drums, combined with their graceful maneuvers and incantations made me feel young again.

All in all, the day of Governor Bradford's marriage to Alice Carpenter was a thrilling one.

~ ~ ~

The *Anne* carried another welcome addition to our community, Bridget Fuller. At long last Deacon Fuller was reunited with his wife. I was almost as happy for him as I was for myself. He walked about for days holding her hand and grinning like a young man as he went about his work.

The ship also brought Lucretia Oldham, a young woman from Derbyshire. She soon become an integral part of our family. The following spring, on April 10, 1624, Jonathan married her. Governor Bradford officiated. As he said the words that officially joined Lucretia into our family, I let my mind wander back to when we first arrived in Amsterdam and Governor Bradford was a young man who lived with us. He was always so appreciative for the friendship William offered him. What a wonder to watch him grow from that young man to assume this role among us as governor. It makes my heart sing to observe him officiating now to make this young woman part of our family.

How blessed I am to live to see my son married by such a dear friend. Two young men, both widowed and both now happy again. Jonathan rarely mentioned the double tragedy of the death of both his first wife and their baby. Neither survived the rigors of childbirth. But on the day he married Lucretia I was as happy as I was distraught the day back in Leyden when both the baby and his wife died.

Truly our lives consist of both deep sorrow and soaring joy.

I looked to the men's side of the church, trying to catch William's attention. He looked at the couple, and I think wiped a tear or two from his eyes. When the service ended, we gathered with the others to celebrate. William approached, took my hands in his, and whispered,

Kathryn Brewster Haueisen

"Weeping may linger for the night, yet joy comes in the morning. Sorrow has turned to joy for both of these young men."

I wondered if he could read my thoughts. Only three years earlier we grieved being separated from Jonathan while Governor Bradford dealt with the blow of his Dorothy's drowning. Life never stays sad or joyful for long. That was a day for rejoicing. By the grace and goodness of God, our whole family, plus a new daughter-in-law, now lived together on the far, far side of the world from where William and I began our own journey. I prayed Jonathan and Lucretia might enjoy a marriage as long as the thirty-three years William and I had shared so far.

Chapter 31

April 15, 1624

Trouble seemed drawn to our fellowship.

Governor Bradford, William, and the others have been challenged trying to keep Lucretia's older brother contained. He seems to care little about any of our ways and is determined to roam as free and unfettered as the wild beasts that prowl the forests.

The joy of a wedding was soon followed by the bitterness of contention.

Unfortunately, the *Anne* also brought Lucretia Oldham's brother John and his wife, another Lucretia, and their son, Christian, to our community. Mr. Oldham came by his own passage, meaning he was neither part of our Leyden fellowship nor sent by the Adventurer investors with a debt to pay back. He soon proved a cause of consternation for the community. Even mild-tempered Governor Bradford considered him malicious.

He felt no obligation to anyone beyond himself, though the Adventurers insisted he must follow the laws of our new colony and serve as needed in military service. For his commitment to do so, he was obliged only to pay the Adventurers one bushel of corn each year. They forbid him to trade with the Indians, though I didn't understand why that would matter. Nor did I understand how the investors expected to know what Mr. Oldham was doing from so far away.

Having little interest in the affairs of the colony, he commenced to stir up trouble with any who were not from our Leyden fellowship. After the numerous challenges we faced on the crossing and in our early months, we had all but removed the differences that first divided us, but now Mr. Oldham seem determined to stir them up again. He stoked resentments among the Strangers. He sent letters back to England filled with false and demeaning stories about our efforts. So sufficiently blended were we by the time the *Anne* arrived, that some days I had to pause to remember who came from Leyden and who joined us in Southampton. All the good relations we forged over the months since we first arrived, Mr. Oldham set about to undo in a matter of weeks. The situation grew worse and worse and no one seemed capable of stopping his destructive ways.

I was especially distressed about all the heartache this caused William. Dear William and others worked hard to build good relations within our settlement.

It alarmed my husband at how easily our love for our neighbors was shaken and broken by just one discontented man.

Mr. Oldham sent letters back to England complaining about us. Evidently the distasteful letters accomplished what he hoped to achieve because in March 1624 an Established Church of England minister, Reverend John Lyford, and his wife Sarah, arrived. We hoped with each new ship we would again see Reverend Robinson, Bridget, and their children.

William was beside himself. "To think our investors send us a minister from the very institution we sacrificed so much to escape. I rather think him a poor substitute for Pastor Robinson."

It was not long before we learned the Adventurers were adamant that Pastor Robinson should never join us. They feared his presence would show too much support for our Separatist ways and cause their power and influence in London to weaken. The day that news arrived I saw William slip out the door of the Common House. I went searching for him and found him strolling around Burial Hill with his chin tucked against his chest and his hands clasped behind his back. He walked slowly, stopping before each tombstone, perhaps offering a prayer for the soul of the occupant of that grave.

He was so preoccupied that I came within a few yards of him before he noticed the small twigs crunching beneath my feet, announcing my presence. He turned and looked at me with sorrow etched on his face.

"We are deceived again! The Adventurers have deceived us again and again. We gave up all we had to establish our own colony where we could establish a caring Christian fellowship. Here rest the remains of those who died trying to create a place where we could live together as we believe the Lord intended we should, and now these . . . these . . ."

I rarely saw William so agitated, and never at a loss for words. His face grew red as an apple and he paced round and round the graves, shaking his fist in the air as he went. Then he regained his composure and returned to the calmer demeanor I knew so well. "Well, what has been done is done. We must conduct our affairs in as godly a manner as we are able and trust our example will result in a good outcome."

~ ~ ~

It seemed there was no escape from the corruption of the crown and the hierarchy of the church. For better or, as it turned out, for worse, we got Reverend Lyford instead of our Reverend Robinson. William had to make do with a letter from his dear friend and colleague. He treasured any word from Reverend Robinson and summarized it for us during an evening meeting. "Pastor Robinson writes that though he greatly desires to be with us, it appears he shall not now, or at any time in the future, be able to join us. We must content ourselves for being with him in our mutual prayers for each other."

When William finished the letter, he sat down with a thud and stared at Pastor Robinson's letter for many long minutes before gently folding it and putting it away in his vest pocket.

Later that day I saw tears glistened on his cheeks. Alone outside after the meeting, he shared his feeling with me. "I fear we shall not see our dear friends again in this life, Mary. Of all the dangers and hardships we endured, this blow seems the cruelest of all."

We walked together along the shore in silence a long time later that day. When he spoke, he tried to put a positive outcome to his disappointment. "What cannot be changed, must be endured. And what must be endured, might as well be accepted. And when we accept what cannot be changed, we might as well find some advantage to the situation."

I agreed but had not yet found any advantage. William already had. "Our lives are far richer for having forged friendships with the Robinsons than had we never known them. We can rejoice for all the benefits their friendship has brought into our lives, can we not?"

I agreed that knowing Bridget had been a great blessing to me. She was not yet dead, only far removed from me. We could still write. With that thought in mind, I set off to do just that, yet still harboring frustration and anger against the Adventurers who had dashed our grand plans. They used our hopes, money and work to establish an English colony and then did what most pleased them, for their own gain, showing no concern or obligation whatsoever for us.

They wanted a colony that represented the ways of the Established church. This they started by the sneaky addition of the Strangers on the *Mayflower*. We integrated this group into ours with kindness and neighborly caring. Then they cared not about our hardship in the ocean passage nor our sickness, but harangued us about our debt immediately. We didn't argue, sending as much as we could back on the second ship. In return, they sent us a spiritual leader of their choosing

Kathryn Brewster Haueisen

and not our own faithful Pastor Robinson. There seemed to be nothing we could do to change this situation. Always able to see some good in any wretched situation, William reminded me, "At least we are governed by our good and trusted friend Mr. Bradford. I thank the Lord for that. And I shall continue to speak to the spiritual needs of our fellowship so long as I have breath to speak. Do not forget, I still am Elder Brewster."

I set to work on a letter to Bridget, leaving William to walk along the beach alone. That always seemed to have a soothing effect on his mood, as it always did on my own disposition.

Listening to water lap the land, sea gulls squalling overhead and seashells crunching beneath my feet always calmed me whenever I felt out of sorts. However, that day it did not.

April 17, 1624

My Dear Friend:

Much to my profound disappointment, we have learned it is not likely we shall ever see one another again in this life. Again, I bid you do not share what I write here with any of the others. I would not have people think me unfaithful or less than loyal to William. Yet, I find myself struggling to answer two questions, which seem the opposite of one another.

I often wonder what kind of wife am I to question the decisions of my husband or to harbor resentment for the outcome of them. I sometimes say things to myself in response to his decisions that is most definitely unchristian and unkind.

Then, at other times, I wonder what kind of mother and friend am I to agree to a plan so outrageous that it could easily cost all of us our lives and certainly has inflicted such great pain in the separation for years from my daughters and now, it seems certain, always from you. My tears well up thinking about it.

Oh, dear Bridget. Do you think I am evil for such thoughts? Do you ever have them? Even as I write this, I am filling up with resentment that I must settle for sending you a letter that will take months for you to read. And many more months for me to receive a response if one is even possible.

It occurs to me that all the lessons I have ever heard about the natural order of things being the husband as the head of the wife, even as Christ is the head of the church have been taught by men. If women were ever allowed to study the scriptures the way men are, I wonder if they would come to the same conclusions.

Now I blush at my boldness. I will close this quickly and seal it. I urge you, do not let others see this. I know I can trust you with the burdens of my heart.

Your loving friend,
Mary Brewster

Kathryn Brewster Haueisen

Chapter 32

April 24, 1624

Governor Bradford has William's way of seeing some good in any bad situation. He says that any reproof to the contentious men in our midst are but as oil to the fire. Yet Governor Bradford says the Lord has brought good out of all this since some who declined to join our Pilgrim church fellowship when they first arrived, decided they would after all. He says it is like the Lord to draw men by unlikely means.

We gradually learned more of the sorry situation of how the Adventurers sent Reverend Lyford when we longed to again see our friend John Robinson in that duty. Some of the story came to us through a letter from Robert Cushman, our fellowship's representative to the Adventurers. He wrote, *The preacher we have sent is (we hope) an honest, plain man, though none of the most eminent and rare.* He further reported that he had made it plain to the investors that our fellowship must consent for him to be our pastor.

The man evidently anticipated the gravity of his circumstance for he disembarked cringing, weeping and bowing in an extreme show of humility. His eagerness to gain our approval was so pathetic it actually elicited a minuscule measure of tolerance for him. After all, he was not the person who refused to send us Reverend Robinson, he did not betray our intentions.

We gave him and Sarah one of the homes for themselves and their children. In a show of good intentions, Governor Bradford went so far as to place him on his Advisory Council. By way of response, Reverend Lyford declared that he had renounced his affiliation with the Established Church!

Many of us chattered excitedly about this.

William remained dubious. "I do not trust that man. There is something about him. Did you note how he never looks directly at who he addresses? And he fiddles with his ring the whole time he is speaking with one of us. I suggest you be careful around that one. He may be like that weasel John Oldham, looking for any small thing to write about to the Adventurers to keep our debt from being paid off in full and set us against each other."

After a few days I agreed telling my husband, "I was watching Sarah. She seemed so . . . it is hard to say. Rather embarrassed or something. She is not particularly friendly if you ask me. She said not a word of gratitude that we gave up one of our homes for her family. But, for the sake of their children, I will do my God-given duty and extend Christian charity to them all."

William's distrust proved correct.

It was not long until the new minister and that rascal John Oldham connived to stir up conflict among us. Before the two of them arrived, we easily overcame any disagreements among us. This we did, in part, out of the necessity of working together to survive, and to a large extent because of the eloquence of speech put to the entire gathering in the Common House by William, Governor Bradford, Deacon Fuller and others.

Kathryn Brewster Haueisen

It seems we can never truly escape contention and conflicts. It was like being back in Amsterdam listening to the English Separatist communities disagree about matters that seemed far removed from what the scriptures taught.

Whenever disputes erupted in Plimoth Plantation, we had nowhere to go to escape. Therefore, we always carefully considered if disagreeing with one another was worth risking the consequences. Though loath to apply discipline, as our Elder, William could chastise people within and without our Leyden fellowship. "I discipline churchgoers with Godly lessons and sharp words if they do not change their ways," he explained to the newcomers.

He always agreed with whatever discipline Governor Bradford deemed necessary. Sadly, discipline was frequently necessary when it came to convincing some of the younger men who seemed reluctant to work. Once my husband tried to use shame to get through to them, explaining how well we got along the first year when we were all working for each other instead of for selfish ends. That talk seemed to have no effect at the time, however the shame seemed to worry them and I think that sermon was the turning point for some of them; knowing older couples had done better than their young bodies at creating this haven.

This matter with John Oldham and Reverent Lyman introduced a new source of contention that would have to be handled in a different way. Fortunately, their turmoil was overshadowed by more pleasurable events.

~ ~ ~

On the 5th of August, 1624, Patience married Thomas Prence. Helping my daughter plan her wedding and what she would need to begin married life was a special kind of honor. It brought on a state of profound satisfaction, like inspecting the first flowers that adorned the fields with the brilliant colors of spring. I was grateful that I lived to fulfill my mission as her mother, to see her safely settled into marriage to a man who would care for her after William and I were gone from this world. Her marriage marked the beginning of a new relationship, one of being longtime friends.

By the time of her marriage, I was moving slowly, with knees and feet that were quick to protest and slow to take me where I wanted to go. I waved away my daughter's efforts to support me as we walked together, but I did remind her to slow down several times. Some days my joints did not feel obligated to do what I bid them do. I found I needed my cane more days than not, though I was loath to depend on it.

We took a long stroll along the beach, over to the brook and back to the sea's shore again. As we walked, I did what I could to prepare her for her wedding night. I presumed she must have questions she did not know how to ask. I knew she must have occasionally observed the mating habits of the livestock, but it was not our way to talk directly about such things beyond discussing breeding for better livestock in the next generation. I remembered my own awkwardness the first night I slept with William. I thought if Patience and I walked enough, she would muster the courage to ask.

Finally, she did.

"What is it like, Mother? Does it hurt?"

The red rising up her neck toward her ears confirmed she was asking about the first night she would share a bed with her husband. I took her hands in mine and gently squeezed them.

"It might hurt. Just a little. At first. But you will soon be carried away in a wave of passion and desire that will distract you from the awkwardness and discomfort. You need not be concerned about knowing what to do. Your husband will show you. What most surprised me was how messy the whole endeavor is. Before you prepare for bed, slip some cloth under your pillow. Then you will be prepared for after, to clean yourself and your husband when you are finished."

Her cheeks turned crimson as she imagined the scene. I hugged her and patted her back. "My darling, you will soon grow used to the intimacy. I hope you will learn to look forward to such moments. It is wonderful when you also enjoy the experience. It is less so if you do not, but your husband insists anyway, especially if a man is impatient and cruel, as some men are. But I think that will not be your fate. The affection of a gentle man is one of a woman's greatest blessings. It is the way of both God and nature. Do not be afraid. Without this, there would be no you. I cannot imagine my life without you and my other children. I pray the Lord will bless you with many children of your own."

I gave her a kiss on the cheek and another hug. I was surprised to feel tears slipping down my checks. I was truly happy for her, but it was yet another large change in my life and there had already been so many of them. As my children claimed their rightful place in the world of adults, my place as their mother became less and less necessary. In the midst of my joy for her, I felt my infirmity tighten its grip on me.

I pushed thoughts of mortality away and forced my stiff joints to carry me back to the cottage to finish wedding preparations.

Governor Bradford presided at their wedding with a simple civil service, as was our custom. Afterwards we rejoiced at having another occasion to set aside our labors for a few hours to celebrate.

Chapter 33

October 15, 1626

Another winter is fast approaching. I cannot believe it has been so long since I last made an entry – evidence that we are now fairly settled. Though I still miss Bridget terribly, I have equally dear and close friends here. My family is with me and growing. Jonathan and Lucretia had their first baby a year ago last March! Keeping up with that busy little baby has kept me too preoccupied to make diary entries.

My dear William continues to pour his heart and soul into providing spiritual milk for our fellowship. Ships come and go now on a regular basis, sometimes bringing good news and helpful cargo; other times only more bad news and trouble. We learned recently that our beloved Pastor Robinson passed away last year. That severs all hope that I shall see Bridget again in this life. William says he believes Pastor Robinson is now in a better place, but I know he misses him more than he has words to speak of it.

I have less and less energy and do not know if I shall make it through another winter, though I pray I shall as Lucretia and Patience are both expecting. A second child for Lucretia. A first for Patience. How blessed we are here in our new plantation home.

I spoke with William often about finding a suitable husband for Fear. I wanted to see her safely settled in a marriage too. I also prayed I would be well enough to participate in the planning of that joyous event. I struggled more each day with pain and often a cough during wet weather. My stomach hurt more days than not, with the area tender to touch. Some days I felt as though a fire was burning inside me. I tried various herbs Deacon Fuller recommended, but none gave me relief for more than a few hours. His wife Bridget frequently sat with me when I felt too weak to do my daily chores. She had a lovely way of quietly putting a place in order without drawing much attention to herself. She and Deacon Fuller together soothed many physical and emotional troubles with their gentle way of coming alongside someone in need of comfort.

Months passed with no suitable husband for Fear. I was distracted in February when Patience confided to me that she was often queasy and had not been able to tolerate more than a bit of hard tack for a couple of weeks. She saw my smile and thought I made fun of her delicate stomach. "My dear, I think you will soon be a mother."

She gasped. "Truly? I thought I had the sickness that sent several to their beds this winter."

I shook my head and inquired if she had other signs that indicated a baby was on the way. "Why, yes. I have been sensitive to smells! Oh, Mother. Do you really think that is it?"

It was!

I was overjoyed at the prospect of soon having more grand-children. By then Lucretia was large with another grandchild and now it would not be long until Patience would also have a child. My concerns about Fear lacking a suitable husband faded into the background when Lucretia delivered a healthy baby girl in March of that year. She and Jonathan named the baby Mary.

She was perfect; a healthy size with a lusty cry. When she wanted something, she clenched her little fists and punched at the air the while howling so loudly we could hear her from our house next door. When Lucretia put Mary to her breast she gulped and slurped for

Kathryn Brewster Haueisen

the first few minutes. Then she would settle down and nuzzle against her. When she was satiated, she sighed with contentment and dozed off with milk drippling down her chin.

Patience safely brought forth her own son a few months after little Mary arrived. He too was a good size and eager to suckle, which gave me hope this child would live beyond infancy, though he was quieter than his cousin. Patience and Thomas named him Thomas, after his father.

My days always brightened whenever Lucretia or Patience brought their babies for me to rock. I was thankful for living long enough to hold a new generation in my arms. I often felt ill and struggled some days to get out of bed. Yet, I always felt better when I was holding one of my grandsons. I caught William smiling as he sucked on his pipe and watched me soothing and rocking a baby. Those moments wiped away all the stresses and sorrows of earlier days.

Thus, the months passed with days filled with simple pleasures. Love and Wrestling grew into young men. Fear and Isaac Allerton spent many hours each day together. When I asked her about it, she was slow to volunteer information and quick to change the subject or excuse herself. Still, Fear seemed captivated by the man, though he was twenty years her elder. And it was time she left us to establish her own home.

My worries about Fear were finally resolved.

In January 1627 Governor Bradford presided over the union of Fear and Isaac. William had misgivings, but he spoke about them to no one other than me. "He seems quick to secure his own position, but I am not confident he considers our best interests in his dealings."

I thought William was perhaps just being overly protective of our daughter. At twenty-six she was well past the suitable age for a woman to marry. Choices in Plimoth were limited. Isaac had been managing his children alone since his wife Mary died only a few months after we determined to establish our settlement here. He was ready to welcome our daughter into his home.

Who knew when, or if, we would ever see another English ship bringing more people to the colony? And I was feeling more challenged by health issues with each passing month. I wanted to see my daughter's future secured. The community had elected him as an assistant to Governor Bradford in 1621. He did the best he could by his children after his wife passed away. There was talk that he might go back to England to work out a settlement plan with the Adventurers for us. What more could a father want in a husband for his daughter?

By the winter of 1626, I stayed in the house most of the time. I was grateful both my daughters were married. I had two grandsons I adored, and Lucretia grew larger each week with her next baby. Thoughts of them warmed my heart, but I could never warm my tender joints. My stomach was upset most of the time and I lived primarily on broths and stews, or food so finely chopped it resembled the food the babies ate.

William was often out of the house, cajoling others to cooperate with Governor Bradford or trying to help resolve troubles with the investors. The Adventurers never seemed content with our efforts. The community determined that sometime in 1627 we should send Mr. Allerton and Mr. Winslow to visit them to come to an understanding. Before that happened, the Adventurers sent people to us to assess our condition. Those people apparently gave unfavorable reports about our efforts, for they continued to send scathing letters suggesting we had deceived them.

I was grateful an ocean separated us. I had no energy left to worry over the situation. Gradually William said less and less about what conversations he had with Governor Bradford and Mr. Winslow. Our time of working to satisfy our debt should be over, yet there continued constant legal haggling over value, time, price and so many other things that I just did not care about at all.

I was content to enjoy my grandsons. I had no strength anymore to even hear about our hard-hearted investors. I trusted William and Jonathan to handle our affairs and I knew them both capable of doing whatever must be done with honor and integrity. I hoped that Mr. Allerton would eventually make some progress in the negotiations, that

Kathryn Brewster Haueisen

appeared to be his strongest area and Fear seemed happy with her circumstance. That was all that truly mattered to me.

A solid fellowship needed all sorts: the spiritual, the hunters, the negotiators, the protectors . . . I was sure Fear's husband would prove his worth in the coming months.

Lucretia and Patience came often with their babies William and Thomas. They were busy little boys and the mothers had to keep a constant eye on them. For little ones just learning to crawl and explore danger lurked in and outside the house. Keeping them from harm was hard for their mothers, as each was expecting another baby. Though I could not do much, I could manage to give them some respite. I want to do more, but the accumulation of all the adventures from Scrooby to Leyden to Plimoth had depleted my energy. It has been a long and overall wonderful life. I have been blessed with a good husband, children and grandchildren with more to come. By April Lucretia appeared ready to have her baby any hour. I was too sick to help much. Patience' baby was not due until fall.

Chapter 34

April 15, 1627

I will complete my account now. My eyes have grown dim and it is more and more difficult for me to write. I scrawl all over the pages now. My children plead with me to tell them stories about their father before they were born. They hear people talking about him and his part in getting us here. It is not his way to heap praise upon himself, though others do so frequently and rather generously.

It is hard for me to remember the years long ago when we were young, full of vigor and dreams. Yet, if I don't tell the children about the legacy they inherit, who will? So, I tell them what I recall between my frequent naps. I hope it makes them proud of him and forgiving of the disruptions foisted upon them by his convictions.

I sensed I would not have many more days on this earth. Yesterday both Patience and Fear came to sit with me. Patience left her little boy with Lucretia, I suppose hoping I would be more inclined to share stories and less tempted to focus on the little boy. They wanted an account of their father's life when he was young. I told them what I could recall.

William grew up in the manor house in Scrooby, because after my father died, his father assumed the position vacated by my father. He always had a curious mind. Some of his relatives saw that clearly and arranged for him to study at Cambridge. But family matters brought him back to Scrooby. If he ever resented not completing his studies, he never spoke of it to me.

Sometimes what seems like a monumental loss, is really only the way forward to a much better outcome. At times the good Lord must lead us through valleys we would prefer to avoid in order to deliver us to a place that is part of his will for us. Because William returned to Scrooby, he was available when Sir William Davison stopped by the manor on one of his regular trips along the North Road. Sir Davison was by then an ambassador to Queen Elizabeth.

As an ambassador he needed an assistant and asked my dear William if he might entertain the idea of taking the position. It was quite a recognition of his potential since he was barely in his twenties at the time. His Cambridge education was sufficient to qualify him for the post, and so began his adventures in diplomatic service. This was all before we married, but I knew of this opportunity and rejoiced with him that it was presented to him.

His service to Sir Davison took him often to London and for a time to the Lowlands, including Leyden. That is part of why our fellowship determined to remove ourselves from the contentions in Amsterdam to establish ourselves in Leyden. William had already spent time there and encouraged the fellowship to consider the advantages of settling there.

Kathryn Brewster Haueisen

I sometimes wonder if William and I should have ever married had what happened next gone a different way.

Sir Davison was promoted to position of Secretary of State for Queen Elizabeth. Her life was in constant danger because her cousin, Mary Queen of Scots, fought her at every turn to return England away from the Established Church and back to Catholicism. Mary's determination and defiance knew no bounds. No prison could stop her conniving with Catholics in Europe. The privy council convinced Queen Elizabeth she must condemn her cousin as a heretic and sentence her to death.

Her majesty delayed and delayed, but eventually signed the death warrant brought to her by Sir Davison. The next day she regretted affixing her signature to the warrant. But it was too late. Sir Davison, under her orders to do so, had the document sealed and delivered. The execution was carried on February 8, 1587

Fearful of the consequences of ordering the death of another monarch, Queen Elizabeth claimed Davison deceived her when he slipped the warrant before her to sign. She also denied telling him to have it sealed and delivered. She sent Davison to the tower, and that brought William back to Scrooby.

Had things not unfolded that way, would we have married? It does little good to speculate how life might have gone should some event resulted a different outcome. We did marry. I was so happy for a few years. William was as good a husband, and father, as any man I ever knew. But he was drawn to the ideas of the non-conformists like a moth to the lantern. I worried that might disrupt our pleasant lives, but never imagined it would eventually make us refugees, fleeing our beloved England to save our lives. And I certainly never envisioned that one day we should all live here! Perhaps the Lord protects us by not letting us see too far ahead on the paths of our lives.

I have lived a life so very different from what I imagined it would be when I said "I will" to William all those years ago in our quiet country village.

The Lord has surely been good to me and I am at peace, waiting to greet my next grandchild.

Kathryn Brewster Haueisen

Chapter 35

April 20, 1627

I take up a pen to complete my mother's diary. Our mother passed quietly into the next world on the afternoon of April 17, 1627 at the age of 58.

Jonathan and Lucretia's little girl was born the day before and they named her Mary, in honor of her grandmother. Mother roused from her sleep long enough to hold her new granddaughter.

She died with Father sitting beside her, stroking her hands with one hand and glancing at the book he held open with his other hand.

~ Fear Brewster Allerton

Epilogue

Jonathan and Lucretia had eight children in all, six after Matriarch Mary Brewster died. They are:

- William (1625)
- Mary (1627)
- Jonathan (1629)
- Ruth (1631)
- Benjamin (1633)
- Elizabeth (1637)
- Grace (1639)
- Hannah (1641)

Jonathan developed a thriving trading business and established a trading post in Connecticut. He died in 1659, Lucretia in 1671.

Patience and Thomas Prence had four children. I did not find exact birth dates for Thomas, Rebecca, Hannah or Mercy. Their son Thomas went to live in England. Thomas Prence was one of the founders of the group known as the Undertakers, formed to finally settle accounts with the Adventurers. Patience died in 1634, a causality of a highly contagious fever that swept through the colony.

Fear married Isaac Allerton and they had one son named Isaac, born in 1630. Fear's husband Isaac was also part of the group trying to settle affairs with the Adventurers and was sometimes accused of doing a poor job of it. According to William Bradford's account of life in the colony, "He screwed up his poor old father-in-law's account to above 200 pounds." Fear also died in 1634, from the same illness that took her sister's life.

Love married Sarah Collier in 1634. Their children were:

- ◆ Sarah
- ◆ Nathaniel
- ◆ William
- ◆ Wrestling

Love died in 1650. I did not find a date for the death of his wife, Sarah.

Wrestling died a young adult without ever having married.

Elder William Brewster died April 10, 1644. His protégé, long-time friend and colleague Bradford was with him to the last.

Governor Bradford later wrote, "He was near fourscore years of age when he died. He had this blessing added by the Lord to all the rest; to die in his bed, in peace, amongst the midst of his friends, who mourned and wept over him and ministered what help and comfort they could unto him, and he again re-comforted them whilst he could. His sickness was not long, and till the last day thereof he did not wholly keep to his bed. His speech continued til somewhat more than half a day, and then failed him, and about nine or ten o'clock that evening he died without any pangs at all. A few hours before, he drew his breath short, and some few minutes before his last, he drew his breath long as a man fallen into a sound sleep without any pangs or gaspings, and so sweetly departed this life into a better."

Kathryn Brewster Haueisen

The four children of William and Mary Brewster who married and had children produced sufficient heirs to fill two volumes of genealogy records through 1907, as recorded by Emma C. Brewster Jones in her two volume *The Brewster Genealogy, 1566 - 1907.*

Though the historical record gives us little information about the life of Matriarch Mary Brewster, she must have been a woman of remarkable faith, durability, compassion, and resiliency.

Approximate Timeline of the Life of Mary Brewster

Historical fiction readers often want to know which parts of a story are factual and which are fiction. With the exception of a few minor characters, the people in this biography once lived, breathed, loved, grieved and struggled just as we do today.

Mary's diary entries are fictional, though based on events that she did actually experience.

Other than a few statements taken from Governor Bradford's written account of life in Plimoth Plantation, most of the dialogue is fiction.

Who was Mary before she became Mrs. William Brewster?

Was she Mary Wentworth, daughter of Thomas Wentworth? If so, she moved into Scrooby Manor twice; once as the daughter of the manor bailiff and postmaster Thomas Wentworth; and again as wife of William Brewster. Or perhaps she was Mary Love (which might explain why one son bore that name). Or perhaps Mary Wyrall. Though some have applied considerable ink defending their theories, no one has yet found conclusive evidence for any of these theories. Was she born in Nottinghamshire? We don't know for sure. Genealogists believe she was born in 1569, based on her stated age as forty years old at the time she and William registered in Leyden in 1609 and buried an infant.

For those who care about the historical accuracy of a story, I present a timeline of Mary's life, based on events researched and recorded by historians and genealogists. Dates are approximate, both because people used a different calendar then than we do now, and because some of the information hasn't been conclusively verified. This is a story; not an academic document.

Assuming she was born in 1569 and her father was Thomas Wentworth, her life would have unfolded like as follows:

Year	Age	Event
~1550		Thomas Wentworth appointed bailiff/postmaster at Scrooby Manor.
~1569	Born	Perhaps to Thomas and Grace Wentworth in Nottinghamshire area.
~1574	6	Leaves Scrooby Manor upon the death of her father.
February 8, 1587	18	Mary Queen of Scots is executed by order of Queen Elizabeth who accuses her Secretary of State Davison of tricking her into signing Mary's death warrant. She sends Davison to the Tower of London, sending his assistant, Wm. Brewster, back to Scrooby where he and Mary reconnect.
1591/2	22	Marries William Brewster at St. James in Scrooby. (Today known as St. Wilfrid)
August 12, 1593	24	Son Jonathan is born, while living at Scrooby Manor.
~1600	31	Daughter Patience is born, while living at Scrooby Manor
~1605	35	Daughter Fear is born, while living at Scrooby Manor.
1606	36	Danger of arrest escalates as William becomes more deeply involved with Separatist leaders. The remnant of Pastor Richard Clyfton's congregation illegally worships at Scrooby Manor after Clyfton is removed from his pulpit for defying King James' edicts.
1607	37	A group of about a hundred Separatists try to leave England. They are betrayed, robbed, and forced to return to Scrooby. William is jailed briefly in Boston, England.
1608	38	The group reorganizes and successfully emigrates to Amsterdam.
1609	39	After encountering conflicts among various English religious refugees in Amsterdam, the Brewsters relocate to Leyden.
1609	40	Mary's infant dies and she declares her age to be 40 at that time.

Kathryn Brewster Haueisen

1609	40	William assumes responsibility for Ann and Robert Pecke, orphaned children of a relative in England.
~1611	42	Son Love is born.
~1614	45	Son Wrestling is born.
1618	49	William opens a publishing business in their home and helps smuggle controversial religious documents back to England.
1619	50	The Dutch, under orders from King James, confiscate all of William's publishing work and seal off the room, sending William into hiding.
1620	51	After a year of managing the household during William's absence, they sail on the *Mayflower*.
March 22, 1621	52	Native leader Massasoit Ousa Mequin calls on the English settlers to negotiate a treaty.
Fall, 1621	52	The famous fall feast, hosted by the surviving English settlers and attended by around 90 Native Americans who had come to check on the safety of their new neighbors.
November, 1621	52	The *Fortune* arrives, bringing a few supplies, numerous single young men, and Jonathan Brewster.
July, 1623	54	The *Anne* arrives, bring Patience and Fear Brewster.
April 10, 1624	55	Son Jonathan marries Lucretia Oldman.
August 5, 1624	55	Daughter Patience marries Thomas Prence.
March, 1625	57	Jonathan and Lucretia's son William is born.
Fall, 1626	57	Thomas and Patience's son Thomas is born.
January,1627	57/58	Fear marries Isaac Allerton.
April 16, 1627	58	Jonathan and Lucretia's daughter Mary is born.
April 17, 1627	58	Mary Brewster slips from this world to the next.

Mary Brewster's Love Life

Kathryn Brewster Haueisen

Acknowledgements

It takes a village to write and publish a book. I am thankful for my now deceased parents Henry C. Hieber and Elizabeth J. Ross Hieber for not only bringing me into this world, but also insisting I be well educated. They encouraged me to explore this wonderful world and instilled in me a curiosity about our heritage. I am also indebted to my mother for her diligent research into our connections to William and Mary Brewster. Her research is the foundation for this book. I am grateful to these people who read the book in very rough draft form and made numerous helpful comments: Sonia Solomonson, Marie Zeller, Nadine Hunt, Bruce Hieber, Linda Schieber, Irmi Wilcockson, Lisa Gillespie, Margery Wheeler, Mary Sohlin Bonnie Reilly, Tassie Hewitt and Elizabeth Splaine.

I am grateful to those who believed this idea for a book had sufficient merit to pursue the enormous effort required to nurture the idea through the lengthy gestation period to completion, and then accompany the book into publication and promotion. The primary midwives for the birth of *Mary Brewster's Love Life* have been publisher and editor, Trish Lewis, cover designer Janet Daghri, web manager Nancy Camden, and promotion guru Mary Walewski. Thank you all. I literally could not have done this without you.

And finally, you dear reader who had enough interest in this woman's story to invest a bit of your time and perhaps your money in learning more about Mary Brewster. I hope her story inspires you to keep going. You just never know where life is going to lead you.

About the Author

Kathryn Haueisen writes about whatever captures her attention.

She became interested, some would say obsessed, in knowing more about Mary Brewster while writing her historical novel *Mayflower Chronicles: The Tale of Two Cultures.* Mary is the author's great grandmother back 12 generations.

That research her led to this book. Haueisen has written or edited six previous books, available through her website and wherever books are sold. She lives the retired life in Columbus, Ohio, where she enjoys reading, writing, researching and stimulating conversations with curious people.

Bibliography

I relied heavily upon the following sources and found them to be the most credible of the many books and on-line data available regarding the Pilgrim Story.

Allan, Sue. William Brewster: *William Brewster: The Making of a Pilgrim*. United Kingdom: Domtom Publishing, Ltd., 2016.

Allan, Sue. *In the Shadow of Men*. United Kingdom, Domton Publishing, Ltd, 2020

Bangs, Jeremy Dupertuis. *Strangers and Pilgrims: Travellers and Sojourners: Leiden and the Foundations of Plymouth Plantation*. Plymouth, MA: General Society of Mayflower Descendants, 2009.

Bradford, William (Paget, Harold, Ed.). *Of Plymouth Plantation*. Mineola, NY: Dover Publications, 2006.

Bunker, Nick. *Making Haste from Babylon: The Mayflower Pilgrims and Their World*. New York, NY: Alfred Knopf, 2010.

Dunbar-Ortiz, Roxanne. *An Indigenous People's History of the United States*. Boston, MA: Beacon Press, 2014.

Fraser, Rebecca. *The Mayflower: The Families, the Voyage, and the Founding of America.* New York, NY: St. Martin's Press, 2017.

Haueisen, Kathryn Brewster. *Mayflower Chronicles: The Tale of Two Cultures.* Brattleboro, VT. Green Place Books, 2020.

Heath, Dwight B., Editor. *Mourt's Relation: A Journal of the Pilgrims at Plymouth.* Bedford, MA: Applewood Books, 1963.

Johnson, Caleb. *The Mayflower and Her Passengers.* USA: Xlibris Corp. 2006.

Johnson, Caleb. Mayflower History Website: http://mayflowerhistory.com/

Jones, Emma C. Brewster. *The Brewster Genealogy, 1566 – 1907* Vol. 1&2. London: Reprinted by Forgotten Books, 2018.

Mann, Charles C. *1493: Uncovering the New World Columbus Created.* New York, NY: Vintage Books, 2011.

Mayflower 400: A Historic Commemoration Website: https://www.mayflower400uk.org

Philbrick, Nathaniel. *Mayflower: A Story of Courage, Community, and War.* New York, New York: Penguin Group, 2006.

Pilgrim Hall Museum, Plymouth, MA Website: https://pilgrimhall.org/

Plimoth * Patuxet Museum, Plymouth, MA Website: https://plimoth.org/.

Russell, Howard S. *Indian New England Before the Mayflower.* Hanover, NH & London, UK: University Press of New England, 2014.

Sherwood, Mary B. *Pilgrim: A Biography of William Brewster.* Virginia: Great Oak Press, 1982.

Wilbur, C. Keith. *The New England Indians.* Guilford, CT: The Globe Pequot Press. 1996.

Winslow, Edward. *Good Newes from New England: A True Relation of Things Very Remarkable at the Plantation of Plimoth in New England.* Bedford, MA: Applewood Books, 1624.

Love Books?

Support Authors - buy directly from independent publishers. This puts more royalty dollars into the pockets of your favorite author - and gives them time to write their next book.

Visit us for links to our other books as well as many other vibrant publishing companies to find the book for you; join our Launch List to be the first to know about new books:

director@vanvelzerpress.com

Van Velzer Press
Americana with a Twist

These ARE The Books You've Been Looking For.

Vanvelzerpress.com

Made in United States
Cleveland, OH
03 December 2024

11290755R00155